Taste Me Deadly

Taste Me Deadly

Nikki Duncan

SAMHAIN
PUBLISHING

Samhain Publishing, Ltd.
11821 Mason Montgomery Road, 4B
Cincinnati, OH 45249
www.samhainpublishing.com

Taste Me Deadly
Copyright © 2014 by Nikki Duncan
Print ISBN: 978-1-61922-416-2
Digital ISBN: 978-1-61922-066-9

Editing by Tera Kleinfelter
Cover by Kanaxa

First Samhain Publishing, Ltd. electronic publication: March 2014
First Samhain Publishing, Ltd. print publication: March 2015

Dedication

To Lisa, who was in my heart and prayers as I wrote this story.

To Slick, for asking the hard questions that make me think on a new level.

To David and Marlena, for helping rid me of hiccups.

Chapter One

Danger had motivated Greycen Craig to leave town. Fear had motivated her to stay away. And guilt had motivated her to return. Her return came with mixed feelings ranging from excitement to worriment and none of them had a thing to do with the curl-frizzing breeze brushing Grey's neck. Instinct tugged at her hands, begging her to twist her now short and darker hair into a knot at her nape. There'd been a time when she'd have died her natural brown-blonde, practically white, and slicked it back in a fierce ponytail. That time was gone so she kept her hands at her sides.

Humidity hadn't been a problem in Vegas, but messing with her hair could reveal her as the once-long-haired woman who'd vanished from Miami five years earlier. A woman who needed to stay invisible, Grey had bent to the will of the U.S. Marshals and long ago given up her ripped and edgy apparel. Mostly. Today's choice of capri pants and a light sweater over a camisole was casual chic. Sweat glued the clothes to her skin, but they were still less stifling than her nerves.

Facing the automatic doors of Miami General, her last conversation with Marshal Micah Carpenter rushed back. His warnings were as adamant in her mind as they'd been in person.

"It could be a trap. Jessup's trial is less than a month away," he'd said. "You're our only witness."

"Maybe you're right. Maybe it is a trap and Jessup's getting desperate." Maybe didn't matter and for the first time in five years—okay, the second—Grey considered leaving WitSec.

"If he is, you're putting Ruby at risk as well as yourself."

"I could be, but I have to do this." She wasn't stupid. Besides, she'd learned a lot about protecting herself through the years. Those years had also shown Grey the kind of person Ruby had always said she could be, and she couldn't turn her back on a lifetime of loyalty.

Grey had met Micah's stone-hard gaze with a daring one. "Did you confirm Ruby's condition, and its cause, with your sources?"

Violence flashed but was quickly controlled. His jaw twitched. "Yes."

"Then she's already at risk." With less than a month before Grey was supposed to testify against a murderer, her sister being in a hit and run wasn't likely a coincidence.

"Grey," Micah had practically growled, as if he didn't know what to do with her enforcing her opinion. "If you go back it's without our protection."

"I'll check in to let you know I'm safe."

"You're not going to find a hero there."

Her shrug had been anything but casual and only invited a more violent look from Micah. He'd argued harder, insisting she'd regret leaving his protection. She'd stood strong despite the doubts he'd planted. The thirty-eight-hour drive that followed had only intensified her doubts until every mile became a twisting pinch of alarm.

The choice to go help Ruby had seemed easy. It wasn't the one she'd have made years earlier, but she'd changed. In part thanks to the help of her therapist. She only hoped it was enough.

Crossing the parking lot, with each step closer to the hospital weighing heavier on her conscience, she worried. Taking chances meant pain, but whose? Hers? Ruby's? Jessup's future victims?

Grey had assured Micah she wouldn't let him down or miss the trial. Her promise to step onto the witness stand, to re-tell everything she'd seen and experienced, was the only thing keeping a cold-blooded, drug-dealing executioner in prison. She'd also made a promise to keep Ruby safe; it was why she'd gone with the U.S. Marshals. Staying away from Miami meant breaking the bigger of the two promises.

Ruby needed help. Grey needed to know if she could be that help. Curiosity and the desire to repay immeasurable debts had pushed her past the limits of the program's safety.

Determined to see her choice through, despite the consequences, Grey continued forward. A little ahead of her, a man helped his very pregnant wife toward the hospital doors. They opened with a whoosh, admitting the couple whose matching wedding bands, smiles and the way they held each other suggested a shared strength that would get them through the new phase of their life together.

She'd dreamed of that kind of connection. Of a family. Briefly.

Rubbing her thumb over the diamond band circling her ring finger, Grey drew in an extended breath and wished for a partner to share her challenges. Having someone to lean on and trust with her secrets might have made things easier, but life hadn't worked that way for her. She didn't have anyone, which made her choices hers.

*

A newspaper article had pulled her from a surreal reality and since there had been no one around to help, she'd taken on the new challenge alone. Grey wouldn't back down. She could help Ruby, make sure she was okay and still make it to the trial. She could do both, and she would.

Inhaling the scent of disinfectant she crossed the threshold and went from heated concrete to gleaming tile. The gleam would end, making way for battered linoleum before long. It was the way hospitals—life—worked.

Angling and turning her neck so it popped, relieving a hint of the tension building there, Grey finger combed the tips of her hair closer to the edges of her face and ducked her head. Shifting quickly from left to right, back and forth, she scanned the surroundings. It was a habit that had become second nature, but she paid more attention to the people than she did to the traditionally sparse decorations in the hospital entry.

Nurses and doctors bustled to and from the cafeteria on the left while visitors moved more leisurely or dejectedly. Volunteers or hospital staff smiled more from habit than genuine warmth as they directed the few people in front of her. No one captured her attention in a way that suggested they didn't belong.

"Welcome to Miami General." A young man who didn't look to be more than eighteen greeted her. "How can I brighten your day?"

Wow. Talk about your greetings that miss the intended mark. Grey was lying low so she bit back the response that would have flown instinctively in Vegas. She kept her head slightly ducked and spoke in a quiet voice that only the boy could hear. "I'm looking for Ruby Donovan."

"Room 420." That he answered without looking at the computer before him tightened the tension in her back.

"You didn't even look that up. Do you know her?"

"No," the boy said, "but a man asked about her yesterday and another one just asked about her a few minutes ago."

Ruby had always been surrounded by people, and she was sexy enough that many of them were men, but they'd never seemed like genuine friends who would visit her in the hospital. Somehow Grey didn't think things were too different now. She'd bet all the sand in Miami she'd just walked into a trap and, no matter how expected, the idea chilled her.

Scanning the lobby area again, skimming past women and anyone not alone, Grey noticed a man sitting by a potted plant. Tall and tan with hollowed-out cheeks, he looked directly past her with an eerily blank stare. He seemed familiar, like she'd seen him but couldn't think of when or where. Razors of agony sliced through her mind—severing her attempt to remember.

Her therapist's advice came back. *The memories will come. When they become too much, envision your safe place and breathe through the pain.*

The woman had sounded like a hippy stuck in the sixties, but she'd helped. Even now, the lessons learned in their sessions helped.

The boy behind the desk was giving her directions to Ruby's room. It took every effort to focus beyond her suspicions and the building headache.

Her sister was the bravest person Grey had ever known, and at the moment she lay in a coma in need of a kidney transplant. Grey's last conversation with Micah played again in her memory as she headed to and waited for the elevator. She'd hoped he was wrong but was now realizing he likely wasn't. If Micah had been right, if Ruby had been targeted and the story in the *Miami Herald* detailing the car accident was part of an elaborate trap, she wasn't sure she'd be able to hide from the danger she'd invited.

The elevator doors opened in invitation for Grey to take the next step. Swallowing, she moved into the square box. The doors were inches from sealing her in alone when a large, dark-tan hand shot inside.

Blunt-tipped fingers. Clean nails and cuticles. The rubber guards smacked against a man's wrist before retreating. The man who'd been sitting alone in the lobby stepped inside, lifted his hand toward the buttons and then dropped it without making a selection other than the one she'd pressed. He leaned back against the stainless-steel wall of the elevator and set his stare on Grey.

Her stomach clenched with ghosts of pain. Her head throbbed.

He was creepy. Intensely creepy.

No longer able to use her hair to veil her face, Grey dropped her chin slightly and fought the urge to press against the wall. She couldn't help but think she'd seen the man before, obviously in Miami. Thinking about it... The razor-sharp pain sliced at her again.

Every instinct she'd trained herself to listen to said he was dangerous. To her and to Ruby. Grey couldn't turn back, but neither could she do anything to jeopardize her sister.

The elevator ding preceded the shaky stop that announced their arrival at Ruby's floor. The doors slid open and though her heart raced with anticipation of seeing Ruby, Grey hesitated long enough to see if the man would step out before her. He hadn't pressed a button for a different floor so he'd have to get off or press a new one.

Paranoia may be setting in, but she wanted to exit second. She needed to know he wasn't following her, though if he was she had few other hopes of shaking him.

Just before she thought she'd have to go first, the man stepped off. When he turned left, thankfully away from Ruby's room, Grey went right. Not ready—or able—to breathe easy, she checked over her shoulder more than once to make sure no one watched her. The man didn't look back. She was still checking after rounding two corners.

At her sister's room, Grey took a bracing breath in the empty hall and pushed open Ruby's door. She'd just crossed the threshold, relieved to not have been followed, when she stumbled to a halt at the sight before her.

The first bed in the room was empty and neatly made. In the second bed, surrounded by utilitarian decor and medical equipment, Ruby lay on white sheets. Bruised everywhere skin showed, and with her left leg and arm in a cast, the only part of her sister that didn't appear battered was her hair. Someone had taken the time to comb smooth her long blonde hair.

Seeing Ruby hurt and in a coma wasn't what shocked her. No. The broad-shouldered and narrow-waisted man sitting in the corner shocked her. His dark-chocolate gaze moved over her. She was certain she read hatred in the depths of the eyes that had once smiled at her. A laptop with the power cord stretching from a nearby plug and a cell phone sat on the table beside him. He'd either been there a long time, or had planned to be.

"Grey." The way he said her name, all smooth and serious with the roll of Scotland on the R made her stomach flip-flop. Damn, the man was delicious.

A masculine voice from down the hall reached Grey and had her closing the door. She hadn't heard the man in the elevator speak, but even if he wasn't following her, the fewer people to see her the safer.

"What are you doing here?"

"Waiting for you."

Except to breathe and blink, Liam never moved. He just sat there with his badge mocking her from its place on his belt. There was no inflection in his voice to convey his thoughts—not that she knew him well enough to read them if there were indicators.

Her left thumb began twisting her wedding band. He was her biggest regret, and now was not the time to unravel the mess she'd made with him. "Why? How?"

"She's beach blonde. You're seductive showgirl." He nodded toward Ruby but he didn't stop staring at Grey. "But even in a grainy newspaper photo, I'd recognize my sister-in-law."

Grey flinched and reached for the hair she'd died so many different colors over the years, before and after leaving Miami. For her return she'd chosen a brown so dark it was almost black. All she could do was smooth the edges along her temple. Avoiding the sun had lightened her skin, and with darker hair she looked paler than usual, but somehow, seeing Liam, she suspected she'd lost even more color.

"So you do remember me." He sounded as monotone as he could with that sexy ass accent of his, but his words were a bitter backhand.

"You're a memorable man." Liam Burgess. Amazing lover. FBI agent. Husband.

"Memorable, but not worth staying with."

"No. Yes. That's not..." She shook her head and took another step into the room. Thoughts fluttered too quickly in and out of her grasp. "Things are complicated."

"Not really."

Liam had been open and easy to be with in Vegas. Now that they were face-to-face he looked pissed. He wasn't going to make their reunion easy. Stiffening her posture and resolve, Grey said, "Yeah. They are."

He cocked his head and a dare danced in the depths of his brown eyes. "We got married, consummated said marriage, you walked. Simple."

"We had so much to drink."

"Not enough to forget getting married."

"No." No. She couldn't say she'd forgotten getting married. Hell, she remembered every detail of the entire night, and she hadn't suffered a hangover the next morning, so she couldn't have indulged in that many drinks.

"You say that like it's a bad memory."

"It wasn't my finest moment."

He flinched. Though she knew he misunderstood, she didn't want to rehash what happened two years ago over her comatose sister. She couldn't stop her curiosity. "Why are you here? Why are you waiting for me?"

"You're my wife, though you clearly wish you weren't."

"That's not... It's not that simple."

"Let me keep this simple then." Liam leaned forward and rested his elbows on his denim-covered knees. The sport jacket he wore over his pricey T-shirt strained across his shoulders. He'd sat the same way in his hotel room when he'd asked her to marry him.

Forward. Intent. Arresting.

She'd blamed the question and her answer on too many drinks in the casinos. The same intensity shone in his eyes now and she felt as weak to resist as she had then.

"I woke up two years ago to find my brand new bride gone. After looking for her, for two years, and trust me when I say I know how to find someone, imagine my surprise when I see her mirror image in a news story."

The same one that had pulled Grey from Vegas.

"A few searches on the victim, Ruby Donovan, and I began putting some of the puzzle together."

Grey twisted the diamond band anxiously as her heart sped. Liam's gaze fell to her left hand. His words bled into one another as he told her about Ruby's blog, where she searched for her sister. Her guilt grew as she listened to him recap his repeat trips to Vegas in hopes of finding her and putting Ruby's mind to rest as well as his own.

"My surprise quadrupled when my searches resulted, finally, in a phone call a couple days ago." Liam hesitated again, locking his gaze on hers, as if making sure he had her full attention. Not that her mind could wander. "I believe you know him as Micah."

Grey swallowed bile. Her knees shook.

Micah had warned her that returning to Miami would have repercussions. She hadn't imagined the undertow would be so strong. Moving farther into the room, closer to Liam, Grey leaned against the edge of Ruby's bed. Her voice, when she found it, trembled with uncertainty. "What did he tell you?"

"Marshal Carpenter," Liam said, impactful, "apologized for blocking my searches."

"He shouldn't have called."

"He cleared me through the director first, who you will be related to as soon as my brother and his fiancée say 'I do'." Liam looked pointedly at Grey's hand and sighed. The sigh seemed to soften him a little. "He said you left WitSec to come here. Then he mentioned Karl Jessup."

Grey flinched. She'd been ashamed to tell the U.S. Marshals what had happened, and that had been a lifesaving necessity. She actually cared what Liam thought of her, so the idea of him knowing everything did not sit well.

In case he didn't know everything she kept her guard up. "I couldn't tell you."

She'd lied, but she'd had zero options. At least not after she'd seen his badge.

"Because you didn't think I'd go into WitSec with you."

"And I couldn't leave it to come back here with you."

"So you vanished."

"So I vanished. Again. And I've regretted it since."

The censure she deserved never came and its absence opened the floodgate that restrained pent-up tension. They may not have a future as husband and wife—she couldn't think about that—but he was here and she could be honest for the first time in five years. Mostly.

The idea didn't free her from the virtual tower she'd been imprisoned in, nor did it reassure her that Liam would be her prince.

Chapter Two

Answers Liam had sought for two years did little to fill the hole Greycen Craig had left in his life. Her presence made all the difference, though.

Sitting guard in Ruby's room for twenty-nine hours had given him ample thinking time. He'd replayed waking alone in the Vegas hotel room, only he'd done it with new information that granted a new perspective. He recalled finding his badge on the bedside table, but saw it now in a new light.

He was from the town she'd been moved from, and he had a specialized skill set that made relocation challenging. He didn't like her choice, or that she hadn't given him one, but he understood. Understanding didn't ease his missing her.

Liam stood and walked the few feet to where Grey sat on her sister's bed. She tracked him with her gaze—piercing blue instead of the honey gold it'd been when he met her.

"Answer one question." The biggest one that continued to plague him even with new understanding.

"Okay."

"Did you regret walking or marrying me more?"

"Marrying you was an impulse I never should have indulged given my situation." She stood and placed her hands on either side of his head. Pushing to her tiptoes she pulled him down and then pressed her lips to his forehead. She'd made the same gesture when she said yes. As it had then, her touch, sweet in its simplicity, eased the anxiety bouncing about in his chest. "I regret that I saw no other path than to treat you like a fling."

So she didn't regret him. The relief he'd dreamed of since that dreaded morning erased the prints of pain. Like a wave-swept beach, his heart was a clean slate. His mind still questioned: was the Grey he'd married real or an assumed identity she would shed when she was safe?

"Grey." Liam lifted his hands, placing one on her hip and one over her left hand. His finger brushed the ring she still wore. His skin absorbed the sensation of her nearness. It was too possible she'd walk again when her business in Miami was finished. "We have a lot to talk about."

"Yes."

He stared into her eyes. Even with her new look, more fragile pixie than shocking seductress, his wife captivated him. Colored contacts held no power against the bravery that breathed fire into her gaze.

"First..." Trailing off, Liam wrapped his long fingers around her hand and pulled her to him. She fell against his chest with a huff.

Creamy chocolate with the slightest hint of pineapple. Sweet. Addicting. Grey's taste was something else he'd thought about. A lot. Driven by dreams, years apart and the danger that hunted her, Liam kissed his wife.

Inhaling her deep into his lungs and soul, he kept his mouth gentle against hers. Her pliancy, moving with and against him, encouraged deeper explorations. A press of his tongue's tip at the crease of her lips begged entrance.

"Liam." Grey parted for him, whispered his name in a way that sounded like surrender. Surrender or relief, something had her shaking in his arms. Or, maybe it wasn't her who shook. It quite possibly could be him.

"I wish you hadn't left, Grey." He reached for the collar of her sweater and tugged the fabric aside. The bare skin, pale as ivory and smooth as his gun's metal, beckoned.

His eyelids dropped as he laid his lips against her collarbone. Cravings he'd suppressed for too long awakened.

Growing desperate, he nipped at the tender skin. She whimpered again and arched into him. His opposite in every way he could recall, she'd brought out a side of himself he hadn't entertained since high school.

He tried to stay gentle, but there was a hunger, an urgency, in him. He returned his lips to hers, caressed her bottom one with his tongue as he shook. His erection pressed against her.

On a moan, she circled her arms around his neck. The kiss simplified the moment, but it complicated the coming hours and days even more.

Liam closed his arms around her waist. Straightening to his full height, he lifted her off the floor as if she weighed nothing. Her feet dangled in the air and images of her legs wrapped around his waist entered his mind. He carried her to the wall, braced against it and then leaned into her.

She opened for him, brushed her tongue against his. Liam needed no other invitation. He swiped his tongue against her, in and out, strong and gentle. She brushed her fingers over his neck and shoulders.

He'd had fun in Vegas and had laughed with her. He'd enjoyed every moment and then replayed each one on a loop for two years. Memories paled beneath the kiss of reality.

Pulling back, Grey angled her head and lightly bit at his neck. He mirrored her. "Damn," she breathed heavily. "You taste good."

"He must," Aidan said from just inside the room.

Liam froze more effectively than any criminal who'd ever been told to freeze. In hopes of staying off their radar, he had told his team he needed a few days off. He'd even been doing his own searches for info on Ruby. Tyler, the team's tech genius, would have been faster but he'd have wanted answers.

Grey tapped Liam's shoulder when he didn't release her. He jolted to action in his head, playing out all the ways this scene could unfold. Unfortunately, they all had the same ending. Prepared for the inevitable, Liam eased Grey to the floor. Before stepping aside, he whispered, "We'll finish this later."

Liam kept a hand on Grey's waist as he turned to face Aidan.

She turned with him and gasped. "You're a twin."

"Yes." No matter how many times Liam had dreamed of making this introduction it had never included these circumstances. "Grey, this is Aidan." Liam rubbed his fingertips on Grey's back instead of swallowing like a coward. "Aidan, this is Greycen Craig."

"Nice to meet you, Grey." Aidan moved close enough to shake her hand. The instant he enveloped her thin fingers with his long ones Liam wanted to pull her back. It was insane, because Aidan was nuts about his fiancée, Lana, and would never consider making a wrong move. Sanity didn't matter against the idea of letting Grey go, if only for a minute.

"How do you know my brother?" Humor played in Aidan's eyes as he looked at Liam. They'd clearly tracked him down through his cell signal or the searches he'd been running. Aidan, more like his journalist fiancée than he'd like to think, had already formulated a story and all that remained was proving or disproving whatever he'd concocted in his head. This had to end before Aidan said too much—like how celibate Liam had been and for how long.

"We met a few years ago in Vegas." Grey thought the vague answer would be enough. She definitely didn't know Aidan.

Liam captured his brother's stare and, with a protective hold on Grey's waist, took the plunge. "She's my wife."

Aidan blinked, scrubbed his left hand's index finger over his forehead, stared. "Your what?"

Doubt surfaced in the light of Aidan's surprise. He should have told everyone about Grey before she showed up.

The question, two stumbling words, conveyed volumes of confused irritation. It was a reaction Aidan normally had toward Lana when she got into a new story, seeming to always be drawn to the dangerous ones. Aidan wouldn't accept the truth easily because for all his bluster, he was a traditionalist.

Protectiveness turned to defensiveness.

Flattening his hand on Grey's back, reassuring himself more than her, he said it again. "My wife."

"Since when are you married?"

"Since the Behavioral Analysis Conference I attended two years ago, but what's important right now is that Grey needs my help."

Aidan shifted his stare to Ruby, and, though he stood still as stone, Liam knew his brother was working to bite back questions. Most days Liam looked forward to swapping verbal spars with his twin. Today was not like most days.

Aidan's shoulders lowered beneath his leather bomber jacket. When he turned his attention back to Liam and Grey he seemed more relaxed. Their mother had always said Aidan carried the hellraiser genes and Liam the peacemaker ones, but since getting engaged to Lana—hellraiser extraordinaire—Aidan was mellowing. The change was especially appreciated at the moment.

"Looks to me like Ms. Donovan's the one who needs help."

"Which is why I'm here." Grey cocked her head defensively and moved to stand between Aidan and Ruby.

Pride burst in Liam's chest. It wasn't everyone who could stand up to Aidan when they didn't know him, but the woman he'd impetuously married had a spine he hadn't seen. Getting to know her could be fun.

"How are you going to help her? You a doctor?"

Grey did not back down from Aidan, instead she made sure she stood tall, which wasn't especially easy given her height. "I'm her sister. She needs a kidney."

"Hold up." Liam interrupted any response Aidan may have had and crossed quickly to Grey. "*That's* why you're here? To donate a kidney?"

"Know your wife real well, I see."

Grey smirked, clearly enjoying her moment. "Guess Micah didn't tell you everything."

"Who's Micah?"

Liam waved Aidan off, not that it would work. His brother was a bulldog. Hell, the whole team was and any one of them would come up with some questions.

"How did you hope to protect yourself if you're under anesthesia?" Liam's demand sounded harsher than he'd intended, but he couldn't ease it any more than he could slow his racing heart. "What if I hadn't been here waiting? Would you have called me? If you'd needed help, would you have reached out?"

"I told Micah I would."

"Which isn't an answer." Liam knew an evasion when he heard one, and he knew the primary reasons for them—

uncertainty and to avoid a lie. He didn't know Grey well enough to know which reason was hers, but he didn't care.

"That's not an answer." If they were at an interrogation table he'd be standing, towering over her. They weren't, though, and he was struggling to keep his cool. She was dealing with a lot, but she wasn't the upfront woman he'd thought her to be. "Would you have called?"

"I don't know."

Aidan moved to the chair Liam had spent the night in and settled. He would have plenty to say about Liam being married but he'd wait and learn more first. It's what he did, just as pretending to ignore him was what Liam did.

"You came here without Micah's protection. Did anyone know you were coming?"

"Ruby's doctor. I called to set up an appointment to talk about donating."

"Did you tell him who you are?" She'd changed her looks, which was smart, but calling ahead could too easily undo that precaution.

"Only my name."

"You think they won't figure out you're sisters when they start doing tests?"

"They ought to see it by looking at her." Aidan spoke more to himself than either of them, but it was the absolute truth. And clearly one Grey didn't want to consider.

Marshal Carpenter hadn't shared any details about Grey's time in WitSec or her connection to the case she was testifying in. Liam could only find so much, but what he hadn't missed was the impression that if Carpenter had known *why* he'd wanted to find Grey he would never have called.

"How do you know this isn't a trap? How do you know Ruby isn't being watched by someone other than me? How do you know her doctor isn't on Karl Jessup's payroll?"

Liam tossed Jessup's name out with the slightest weight added. He'd given Aidan a crucial piece of information, but more importantly, the tiniest flicker of her eyelids evidenced that he'd hit his mark with what he knew. She'd considered the same possibilities.

"I don't know any of that, but how do you know I haven't given this proper consideration?" she challenged.

"I hope you have, because while I get wanting to help Ruby, you need to be smart about it."

"I'm smart." Grey rested her hands on his waist and looked into his eyes. The connection weakened his resolve to argue. "And you're already here so we don't have to worry about what I might have done."

He really hated evasiveness, hers more than most because it did nothing to ease his suspicion. The biggest one being that she wouldn't have reached out, or if she had it would have been too late.

"Well, since I am here and you need protection, you get to play by my rules."

"Depends on your rules."

"The ones that keep you and Ruby safe while allowing you to be here for her."

Aidan's cocky grin stretched his mouth, probably because he knew how fast and flat that demand would fall if directed at any of the women in their lives. Grey was different. Her circumstances were different. She was used to living under restrictive dictates, and unlike the U.S. Marshals, Liam offered something she wanted.

"I'm going to need a few more details," she insisted.

"You had zero details when you left with Micah. I'm not going to take you away from your sister."

"Yes, but your deal sounds as if I'm going to have a babysitter twenty-four seven."

Liam nodded. "Because you will."

"Then no deal."

Aidan laughed. "Oh, she's going to fit in nicely with the girls. Especially Lana."

Liam turned on his brother, who was obviously enjoying seeing someone else fight a willful woman. "You're not telling anyone else about her. Even Lana."

"Lana's going to know I know something. Woman's a damn savant like that," he muttered. "And you're going to have to tell the rest of the team at some point."

"Yes, *I* will tell them."

Aidan leaned forward and braced his elbows on his knees so his hands dangled. It was a stance they both took often and they were rarely as relaxed as they looked. "Let's see if I've pieced this together correctly and then maybe you'll let me help."

Grey shook her head. Liam didn't bother.

"And you accuse Lana of being pushy." Any attempt to stop Aidan from hypothesizing would be wasted so he gave it no energy.

Expectedly, Aidan ignored him. "You found yourself in some kind of danger that drove you into hiding. Now, your sister is hurt so you've left your safety net—I'm guessing his name is Micah—and you need my brother, your husband, to watch out for you while you have and recover from a surgery."

"If I qualify as a donor. And I can protect myself."

Aidan shrugged off her argument and indulged his preference for facts and things he could control. "What I haven't figured out is who Micah is. Can't be a brother or you'd have left him behind with Ruby. Judging by the kiss I walked in on, and hoping for the best in a sister-in-law, I don't think boyfriend."

"Is he always so—"

"Annoying?" Liam finished for Grey as he stepped up to stand directly in front of her. Locking his gaze with hers he tried to ignore Aidan.

"Yes," she said with a sigh.

"We Feds like our puzzles. Aidan's missing a lot of pieces." *So am I.*

"The biggest piece is when you two got hitched. Before, during or after you went into hiding. It's obvious you're into each other, so for you to stay apart I'm guessing after the danger and during the hiding."

Liam ran an index finger over her stomach, wishing they were alone and naked but settling for what he could get. "You may as well tell him. Or let me."

"The fewer who know the better."

"Do you trust me with what I know? Do you trust me to watch out for you and Ruby?"

An instant and resounding yes would have been nice, but she took her time with the answer. Her hesitation and consideration lent credence to whatever she'd say. "I do."

The whispered words whipped him back to Vegas and had him smiling as broadly as he had that night. He wouldn't let her down. In fact, he'd do everything possible to win a second chance after the threat to her life was gone. "Then trust me when I tell you I'll only bring in people I trust with my own life."

"And you trust Aidan."

Liam nodded. "Plus a few others."

Eleven others to be exact, and though they didn't all see each other daily they would all circle around Grey and Ruby with fists and weapons at the ready. When they heard she was his wife they'd grow especially protective.

"Fine." Her shoulders dropped. "Tell them."

Chapter Three

Grey picked at the Band-Aid that pulled the fine hairs on her arm. The cotton ball beneath the tan strip was intended to apply pressure and stop the bleeding faster. It applied pressure. Everything since reading the hit-and-run article about Ruby applied pressure.

Her sister was in a coma and could die.

Pressure.

The U.S. Marshal who'd kept her safe suspected a trap.

Pressure.

Her FBI husband had found her.

Pressure.

She needed protection but had left WitSec.

Pressure.

Liam was asking her to trust him and his friends.

Pressure.

The vein that had already given body-weakening quantities of blood. throbbed. A bruise spread around the Band-Aid and darkened the skin of her inner elbow. Her entire arm ached, but, perversely, she preferred it to feeling nothing. With only a brief respite two years ago, she'd lived a numb existence for too long and while she wasn't thankful for Ruby's accident, she was grateful for the changes it forced in her.

Opening the door of the exam room with a stack of pamphlets and forms in hand, Grey found Liam leaning against the wall with his arms crossed over his chest. Not all the changes filled her with thanks.

"Liam."

He fell silently into step beside her as they headed for Ruby's room. His arm brushed hers, or rather, the sleeve of his jacket did. No skin touched and no intimacy was intended, but she felt it.

He'd asked for her trust, which had been easier to give than she'd expected. Then he'd said he wanted to bring his team, his friends, in. That was when things got dicey.

She could count on one hand the number of people she'd trusted in the last twenty-nine years. She'd even have fingers left over. Liam could practically fill a notepad with his list and he wanted her to blindly trust them.

It was more than she'd expected or thought herself ready for.

"How'd it go?" Liam asked as they entered the stairwell, hushing the hospital sounds behind them.

"Fine. Why aren't we using the elevator?" They'd used the stairs earlier too.

"Always have an escape plan, Grey. Elevators are traps."

It made sense, especially when she recalled how she'd felt sharing the elevator with the man earlier. Cornered. Threatened.

"Did the doctor say when they'd have test results?"

"Tomorrow hopefully. They're putting a rush on them given Ruby's condition." Grey lifted the papers she'd been given. Wincing when the move put pressure on the bruise, she ripped off the Band-Aid. "While I wait I have homework and an appointment for a psych evaluation."

"Is that such a great idea?"

"A psych eval?" She dropped the bandage and cotton ball in the trash can as they turned for the next level. "I can't exactly avoid it."

"I can't imagine they'll go easy with the questions."

"Your concern is touching, Liam, but I don't have a family history of mental breakdowns to worry about." And I'm not a stranger's to a therapist's couch.

His eyes crinkled a tad, suggesting the tiniest of smiles might grace his mouth. The man had a beautiful smile. "You know that's not what I mean. I'm not fishing for secrets."

She shrugged, but said nothing.

"I worry that the questions, how you answer them, will bring danger closer."

"You're seeing conspiracies where there are none. Jessup's a murderous ass, but he's not powerful enough to have the hospital staff in his pocket."

Grey brushed her fingers over Liam's, curling the tips enough to create a hook of sorts. She stopped, maintaining her touch. He turned and faced her with a look in his eyes she couldn't quite decipher. Then he quirked a brow in a way that deepened the vertical line in his forehead. He was intense, but the line made him approachable, because it showed her his concern when his words didn't.

"Besides, I've had five years to perfect the art of a lie."

"So I shouldn't believe anything you say?"

"The only lie I ever told you was my name." Nerves set in and had her fidgeting with Liam's fingers.

"As I recall, you never told me anything more." He squeezed her fingers gently. "Now, seeing you as a devoted sister willing to risk herself and remembering the vivacious mystery woman from Vegas, I find myself growing curious."

"About?"

"Which woman is the real one?"

"Is a stairwell really the place for marital confessions?"

Without releasing her hand, he set his free hand on her waist and backed her toward the banister. "It's a safer alternative to what I've wanted to do with you since you walked into Ruby's room."

Her heart pumped faster. The taste of unquenched passion from earlier lingered between them. Grey swallowed. "Your alternative to the alternative is pretty tempting."

"Greycen Burgess, *you* are the temptation."

Greycen Burgess. With two words that sounded distinctly intimate Liam doused her in ice. Moving up a step, she eased away. "Grey Craig," she corrected.

The line in Liam's forehead creased again. His eyes twitched at the corner. "We're married. Using my name could add a layer of protection."

"Not really. It just connects me more closely to you, which would tell Jessup's people exactly where to look." Regret set in and immediately had her wanting to retract her argument. That had sounded like an assumption she'd be staying with him. Talk about dangerous. "We should get back to Ruby."

"Aidan wouldn't have left her alone."

She looked over her shoulder as she moved ahead of Liam on the stairs. "While I appreciate his help I don't want to rely on a brother-in-law I don't know or your friends who have no reason to care."

"They'll care because I care."

That was the exact logic that didn't compute. What kind of people took someone in just because a friend asked them to? If Liam had those friends it had to say something about him as a man. To Grey, it said he was the kind of man she should never have said "hello" to, let alone "I do".

"Don't you have jobs? How can so much of your time be spent here?"

"I have vacation time coming."

"And Aidan?"

"He's working. Thanks to technology we don't have to be in our office all day to do our jobs."

"It has to be easier, though."

"We're in the field more than you might think." At Ruby's floor Liam opened the door and checked the hall before allowing Grey to pass. "You said I could tell them. Are you trying to get rid of us?"

"Of course not!" She squeaked louder than she'd intended.

"That was convincing."

"I'm sure your ego can survive the hit."

"But can our marriage?"

Their marriage, if it could be said they really had one, was a topic best discussed later. Much later. "What happened in Vegas really should stay in Vegas."

"Shouldas, couldas and wouldas tend to follow us until we deal with them."

"Ours are going to have to wait a little longer." Grey pushed open the door to Ruby's room. A wall of white-coated men and women surrounded Ruby. Aidan stood by the head of the bed looking fiercely protective.

An older woman, clearly the one in charge, explained Ruby's injuries. They launched into a discussion about treatments and recovery times.

The white coats blurred. The walls trembled and moved in, shrinking, depleting the oxygen levels. Grey tried to focus on what was being said about her sister, but nothing penetrated. There were too many people. Ruby was vulnerable. Grey was vulnerable.

She'd made a habit of avoiding crowds and this was a faceless one that could hide a killer.

Sound buzzed. Heat spread. Dizziness swarmed. She recognized the signs of an approaching panic attack and knew there was no stopping it. She swayed.

The papers slid from her hands.

Liam's large hands landed on her waist an instant before she collapsed against him. Carrying her as much as he supported her, he led her to the bathroom and closed the door behind them.

The confined space was no better than the crowded room. There was no escape and one of Jessup's people could be out there. Grey shook with her uselessness.

Liam turned her to face him, but he offered no platitudes or advice on calming down. Wordlessly he wrapped his arms around her, held her close. Instinct said to fight, to resist. Then his warmth penetrated the chill of terror. His steady heartbeat encouraged hers to match its pace. As smoothly as he could lead her across a dance floor he was leading her from a scary abyss.

"I should have stayed in Vegas. Gotten Micah to help coordinate this long distance."

"That might have been safer."

"Or it could have drawn someone to me and no one would be here to watch Ruby."

"So you're glad we're here."

"And in case I forget to say it, I appreciate the protection." It was the only admission she could afford. Her resistance, at least for the moment, was gone, because the whole situation was an emotional blender capable of stealing dreams faster than Jafar.

Hours had passed with Grey reading pamphlets and Liam doing research on organ donation. They talked about small things like Grey's life in Vegas and they argued over what to watch on TV—not that Liam cared what she watched as long as she was there.

"It makes sense for you to stay with me." Liam turned toward his car.

"It's not right." She cut toward hers.

He took her hand and pulled her behind him. "We're married. Spending the last two years apart wasn't right."

"We barely know each other." She pulled free and turned, again, toward her car.

He reached out and grabbed her hand, again stopping her. "Which we need to remedy."

"Not by living together while I'm in town." She stepped back, shook her head firmly.

The tug-of-wills game they had been playing since he suggested she stay with him had reached ridiculous levels. Grabbing her hand again, this time more firmly, he turned her to face him. "What are you really afraid of, Grey?"

"Nothing."

"Bullshit." He gave her no time to react before continuing. "Whether you're afraid of Jessup or facing me alone, something's got you scared."

"Then it must be Jessup, because you don't scare me."

"That's convenient for you." Her head dropped at a slight angle to the left. He went on. "You scare the shit out of me."

Her lack of a quick quip painted a smile on his heart. She was as unsure of them as he was. Preying on her momentary weakness, he led her to his car.

The idea of learning they were incompatible in the real world scared him.

The idea of realizing he'd been faithful to a woman who wanted nothing to do with him scared him.

The idea of losing her again, more than anything else, terrified him.

He was opening the passenger door of his car when she pulled her hand away. "I can drive myself."

"You could." He pointed to the waiting seat. "You're not going to."

"Liam." She dropped a hand on the doorframe and met his stare. "There's protection and then there's overbearing. You're crossing the line."

He again pointed to the seat, this time dropping his head to acknowledge her point. "You're right."

Grey nodded and slipped in. Round what-the-hell-ever-number-they-were-on was happening on his turf.

Liam slid behind the Chrysler 300's steering wheel, loving as always the way the SRT8 seats hugged his sides. He spared Grey a quick glance as he started the car and pulled out of his spot. The look on her face—satisfied victory—made it clear she expected him to go to where she'd parked. He instead left the hospital.

"Hey! My car."

"Will still be there tomorrow."

"You said I could drive myself."

"And I still think you could. If I'd let you."

"Of all the overbearing, chauvinistic…"

"Asshole ways to behave," he finished for her. Pleasure had him wanting to grin. Self-preservation had him holding back. He was picking a big enough fight by ignoring her. Flaunting the perverse fun he was having would only amplify her anger. They were going to learn about each other under strained circumstances and he knew himself well enough to know his easygoing side would only dominate for so long.

"I liked you better in Vegas." She crossed her arms and slumped into the seat.

"Me too."

"Then act more like you did then."

He reached over and untucked her left hand. Lacing their fingers, he raised her hand and kissed the back of it. "Until we know you and Ruby are safe you're stuck with this version of me."

Looking at the hand he held, her cheeks flushed pink. She chewed on her bottom lip, clearly worrying over what to say or do. She could say anything she wanted, though. He wasn't giving her many choices on what to do.

"Are you sure Tyler will stay all night?"

"You heard him. He has no one to make demands on his evenings."

"I heard him." She shook her head. "I also noticed he barely looked up from whatever he was doing on his tablet."

Now Liam did smile. Most people couldn't say what color eyes Tyler had because he so rarely dragged them from his tablet or computer. It didn't make him less aware of his

Nikki Duncan

surroundings and the people in them. "I guarantee he can recall and describe every person and moment in his day."

"How? He never looks up."

Liam shrugged. "I stopped trying to figure it out. It's more fun to watch people underestimate him in that regard."

"I still should have stayed the night."

Liam squeezed her hand in a gesture of support and understanding he hoped she'd accept. "I get that, but you're trying to be accepted as a living donor."

"So?"

"So, having a little support through the process couldn't be bad."

"I'm fine on my own."

"When's the last time you slept? You drove over thirty hours, only stopping for gas, and you've been at the hospital for twelve hours. By my calculation you're working on two days."

"I guess I am a little tired." Falling victim to the suggestion, Grey gave a large, jaw-popping yawn. "Though I'll be surprised if I really sleep."

"How about food? It's been a while since that cafeteria lunch."

Her stomach rumbled in answer. She shook her head and pinched her lips tightly. She may argue that he'd acted heavy-handed by driving and insisting she stay at his house, but he was trying to take care of her.

Awareness moved around her in the way her shoulders shifted back and her chin rose as he pulled up to the security gate at his division's entrance. "You've got to be kidding me."

He smiled before rolling his window down to greet the security guard.

"Good evening, Mr. Burgess." The older man leaned against the door window. His arthritic swollen fingers shook against the frame.

"Mr. Lambert. How are you?"

"Old and tired." Mr. Lambert smiled at Grey. "You don't get many ladies for company. Who's your friend?"

"This is Grey, my wife."

"Liam," she moaned. "Stop doing that."

Mr. Lambert laughed. "What did you do? Elope? Is that where you've been the last couple days?"

"Something like that." Liam winked and then grew serious. "Do me a favor, will you?"

"Sure."

"If anyone comes by asking for Grey or claiming to know her, let me know. Right away."

"She got trouble?"

"Maybe. Just taking precautions."

The other guards who worked the gate wouldn't have left it at that, but Mr. Lambert had spent his adult life in the Marines and then Miami P.D. A Homicide retiree, he'd seen some of the ugliest parts of life. He and Liam had shared enough bonding beers in the clubhouse for the man to know Liam wouldn't make the request unless it really mattered.

"I'll call your cell and make sure the others know to do the same."

"Thank you." Liam said his good-byes and drove toward the opening gate.

"Don't you think that's a little over the top? And I'm actually *not* referring to yet another intro as your wife."

"You *are* my wife."

"It's just a piece of paper."

"One that will give you extra protection and benefits without explanations."

"Why couldn't you just say I'm a friend?"

He'd known things wouldn't be easy, that they had everything to learn about each other. Exhaustion clung to them both so he was working hard to hold back the bite that came too easily when he got tired. Exhaustion topped with her fighting him at every development bordered a thin line laced with gunpowder. One wrong comment would spark the match.

"You're more valuable as my wife. And it halts wagging tongues faster."

"Instead of wondering where we met and if we're having sex they're wondering when we got married and where I've been."

"But I'm more inclined to fight for a wife than a woman I'm dating. Trust me, it's easier to be upfront and say you've been living out of town."

"Bullshit." She used the tone he had earlier and, like he had, she continued before he could say anything. "Whether you're lying to yourself or to me, your logic's missing."

"Only because you don't want to see it, Grey." She was family. No one messed with his family.

Chapter Four

Whatever argument she'd thought to make fell away when he turned into a driveway. Being in a gated community with a security guard instead of a code pad had been her first clue that he had money. Then there were the houses. Immaculately landscaped and grand. Still, a part of her had kept hoping he was pulling a prank or that it was a safe house. Anything was better than thinking he really expected her to stay where she didn't belong.

And she hadn't belonged in a place like his house on the best day of her life.

The car rolled down a long drive that forked off from a circle at the front to go straight to the back of the house. The stamped design that left grooves in the concrete made a brick road sound beneath the tires that bumped lightly over them. She hadn't noticed Liam pushing a button, but as he rounded the back corner of the house the garage door was reaching the top of its track.

The three-car space had been finished and painted, but not so much that the heavy support beams had been covered. Dark, glossy wood contrasted with bright gray walls. Just as the project sitting on the workbench seemed to be waiting, recessed lighting waited overhead. Tools, tidily hanging in straight rows, gleamed with the shine of newness.

"Do many projects here?"

"Yes." He came to a stop beside a white, two-seater convertible that looked more like a chick car than something

Liam would drive. "I was taught to do things myself around the house."

"Clearly you can afford to pay people."

"Everyone says that."

She turned, mouth agape, and shook her head. How could he pretend surprise that people would think he had money?

"Okay, yes," he conceded while turning off the car and pressing the button to lower the garage door. "I can afford to pay for any repair needed; I wouldn't have bought the place if I couldn't."

"But?"

He leaned across her, holding her gaze for a moment when his nose was close enough to brush her. "But I'm able to afford them and this place because of the money I save doing the work myself."

He opened her door and leaned back, unconcerned with whatever she might argue next. The man made no sense. "This is more than a few dollars saved on odd jobs."

"There was also an inheritance that did well on some stocks. And it could be said I got a killer's discount. A financial trifecta." He nodded toward the house. "Come on, I'll show you around."

"A killer's discount?" Questions and uncertainty flailed in her mind. His jacket was high quality and his car had every gadget possible, but she'd never have guessed he lived in such a high-end place. He came across as so normal.

"The place was seized in a prostitution and murder investigation we worked. It made it a tough sell." He led her through the laundry room, that was an actual room, and into the kitchen. She was struck again by the magnitude of contradictions that surrounded him. Her heart raced.

Massive, the room boasted a large refrigerator with double doors and a freezer drawer below, a gas cook top with six burners and a griddle, double ovens and an oversized microwave. The main cabinets were white with black marble counters and, for contrast, the island, giant in its own right, had ebony cabinets topped with white marble.

Like the garage, the walls were a pale gray with dark beams exposed. Color, bold blues and greens, popped to life from the trinkets and artwork, as well as from the centerpiece bowl filled with fruit, and the eight barstools surrounding the island.

Her inner cook, the woman too rarely released in the last five years, rejoiced at the kitchen's splendor. Her inner chocolatier, another part of herself suppressed years earlier, longed to see smoothly melted chocolate being worked on the white marble. She rubbed her fingertips together, practically feeling the silk of chocolate between them.

The only thing that might be better than a cooking indulgence would be to settle onto a barstool with a glass of wine to watch Liam cook. Assuming he cooked.

She ran her fingers along the edge of the cool marble as she followed him into the living room. The gray walls and exposed beams continued. The same blues and greens from the kitchen greeted her from wall hangings, the pillows on the leather sofa capable of seating ten people, and the enormous rug that covered the beam-matching hardwood floors.

She didn't need to see the rest of the house to know it would be equally awesome. And equally out of her league. "What does a single man need with all this space?"

"I have company quite often. And I'm not single." He continued down a hall and into the main entrance, giving her a glimpse of the formal areas before turning up a massive staircase.

"Enough company that you need all this space?"

"I have a large family."

An image of overbearing Scots filled her head. It was powerful enough to make her cringe. "I'll be sure to be gone before they come back."

"My team and their significant others also come over often."

"How many of them are there?"

"There are six of us on the team, four of them are either engaged or married, well, five if you count me, one of the fiancés has a sister and then we have another friend who stops by when he's in town."

"So there are twelve of you in your little group."

"Thirteen."

She did the math again and shook her head. "Who's number thirteen?"

"You."

"What?" She stumbled. "No. I'm not joining your merry little band of whatever you all are."

"Sweetheart." He stopped at the first door in the upstairs foyer and pressed a kiss to her temple. "You're already a member."

"Liam, I hope you're not expecting this *thing* between us to last."

"I have just as much reason to think it will work out as you do to think it won't."

"I don't even know how to respond to that."

"Then don't try." He leaned around her and opened the door they stood beside. His arm brushed her breast and set tingles racing through her. She lifted a hand, set it on the back of his forearm.

His jacket felt creamy against her fingers. He angled his head, met her gaze.

So many things needed to be said, discussed. She owed him an explanation. He deserved to know why she'd left, to know it had nothing to do with him. The trouble was that she'd leave again when Ruby was safe, so anything she said would be little more than empty platitudes.

"Liam."

"Grey."

They spoke at the same moment and they both sounded out of breath. Screw explanations. If burning in Miami's fiery pits of despair rested in her near future she may as well enjoy the trip.

Curling her fingers into the back of his arm she leaned into him. Slow and dreamlike, Liam eased forward. Grey pushed up to her toes and touched her lips to his. It was a tentative touch and she kept her eyes open, locked on his, not that the thoughts behind the brown shields to his soul were readable.

Retreating, she swept her tongue across her lips. Liam placed a hand on her stomach and pulled at her shirt. He made no move to untuck it, yet each tug pulled on the yearning to belong that breathed inside her. Then she grabbed his jacket and began to pluck at the fabric.

"This is wrong," Grey whispered, more for her benefit than his, a way to remind herself how things would end. She didn't belong in his world that was resplendent in perfection. She didn't know how to be the kind of person he surrounded himself with, openly supportive and instantly loving. She was more comfortable in her one-bedroom apartment filled with mismatched furniture that could only be called shabby chic in a dream. Differences aside, she had no desire to be involved with someone tangled up in the law. Either side.

"Seems right to me." He breathed a kiss across her lips again. Nothing more than a rush of warmth backed by the lightest caress of softness, the kiss sent her rationalizations scurrying for cover.

"Things are complicated."

"Easy is boring." He kissed her again.

Her knees trembled. Her other hand drifted up and grabbed the front of his jacket. "Boring is safe."

"Safety and excitement can dance on occasion." His next caress was a nibble kiss at her jaw, just in front of her ear.

She licked her lips and tightened her hold on his jacket. He unraveled her restraints. "What kind of dance?"

"The oldest kind." Demonstrating, he gathered her close and began to move. They stood in a large foyer at the top of the stairs with no music playing and he was luring her into a dance.

Then she heard it. Music, deep and throbbing like a heavy heartbeat. The stunning strains of sweeping notes played in each touch. His palm at her hip. A finger at her throat's pulse.

Her blood hummed. Desire swelled.

Applying almost no pressure, he moved her hips forward and back, wrapping her in warmth and comfort and arousal. Grey rested her temple against his jaw and craved the strength to allow herself to be carried away.

Complications underscored Liam's efforts to simplify the moment. Grey just didn't know how to accept the simplicity.

"I can't." Lifting her head she forced clarity into her mind. The fog of fantasy lingered, though.

Liam surprised her when instead of arguing or ignoring her, like he did every time she insisted his help wasn't needed, he set her down. She wasn't sure when he'd picked her up but the instant his hands released her she missed them.

"Do you promise not to run away in the middle of the night?"

"Are you really that worried about my safety?" The idea of him caring enough to worry was novel, which was nothing more than a dream she couldn't entertain.

"Yes, but let's not pretend you haven't mastered your disappearance act."

Guilt, an emotion she'd once thought she squashed, showed its traitorous head, which it seemed to be doing a lot lately. It had been bad with Ruby, yet standing in Liam's home it mixed with regret and overflowed.

"My promise probably means nothing to you, but I will not leave in the middle of the night."

"Good." He leaned in and kissed her again. This time it was almost chaste, as if he was simply saying "good night, sleep tight", but as she breathed easy he tugged her bottom lip between his teeth, swiped his tongue over the puffy spot she'd made bleed earlier with chewing nerves, and then pulled back.

He pointed to the end of the hall. "I'm just around the corner if you need me."

Her knees shook as she watched him walk away. She'd been so certain he would seduce her into his bed. The weekend in Vegas had been the first and last time in five years she'd slept dream free and the prospect of repeating the pleasure was stark.

He was rounding the corner when she called out. "Liam."

He turned but said nothing.

Grey was tempted to shake her head and go into the room. Retreat would be cowardice. Cowardice would mean sleeping in the nude, which she refused to do. At least in Liam's house with him down the hall. "My stuff is in my car. I have nothing to wear."

He looked her up and down. Hunger rolled over her and had her wondering if he pictured her naked. Her mouth watered.

"Your bag is in your room."

"How?"

"Tyler moved it while you were in your appointment."

Her hand went to the pocket where the single key was. Had been. Skin hot and tight, she said, "You picked my pocket."

Liam's only move was the slightest shrug with one shoulder.

Her skin heated more. "You planned on bringing me here from the beginning."

"You're my wife. You belong here, even if you prefer not to share a room with me." Offering no other explanations he pivoted on the ball of his left foot and walked away.

Heart heavy, Grey went into *her* room. Her doubts followed.

Unlike the downstairs that started with pale palettes, the bedroom was brilliantly bright. The walls were teal green, but one had been painted with fat lines in a slightly darker teal. Baseboards and crown molding as glossy and smooth looking as white chocolate added elegance the space didn't really need.

The bed frame, tables and dresser were the same color as the molding, but the bedding, seating area chairs and decorations pulled in shades of teal with touches of pink. On the floor at the end of the bed sat her brown bag with its slight tear at one corner.

Standing in a bedroom that could fit her entire apartment, Grey was surrounded by perfection and wealth. Liam was going out of his way to welcome her. He'd offered protection, privacy, comfort and no pressure in regards to sleeping together. She should be grateful, and she was, but every gesture was shadowed by reality.

Fed or not, married or not, Liam did not need to take on her problems.

She'd promised not to leave in the middle of the night, and she'd meant it. She'd thought she would stay, but looking at the clock, seeing that it was nearing midnight, she knew differently. Hands cold and shaking, she wrapped her fingers around the handle of her bag.

She was out the door and down the stairs before his earlier words smacked her back a step. *Let's not pretend you haven't mastered your disappearance act.*

Grey spun, expecting to see him descending the stairs. He wasn't there. Shaking off the idea of being watched, she turned for the front door. She turned the first deadbolt. Her fingers were on the second.

"Unless you're leaving Ruby again, too, I'll track you down in a few hours."

She'd never been easily startled or prone to screams, not even when she was moments from being discovered by Karl Jessup, but she felt one rising. Closing her eyes, Grey froze, unable to face Liam. "I can't be here."

His fingers encased hers on the bag. She flinched. Where had he come from and how did he move so soundlessly given his size?

She wouldn't ask any more than he'd answer if she did. "Why, Grey? Why can't you be here? Why do you keep running?"

He took her bag and without its weight in her hand she lost the resolve she'd barely been gripping.

"Your world is too different from mine." She hated the squeak in her voice, but she went on. "My apartment can fit in that bedroom."

He relocked the door and then, taking her hand in his, led her back to the stairs. They were at the top landing before he finally spoke. "You're judging the book cover. This is just a house chosen because it's big enough to accommodate my family without us tripping over each other when they visit."

"Ruby's my only family."

"It doesn't have to be that way." He led her past the teal room, past a few other doors and around the corner he'd turned earlier.

He was going to his room. She tugged at her hand but he didn't grant the freedom she sought. She'd made a promise and decided to break it in a span of five minutes. He had as much reason to trust her as Thor did Loki.

Chapter Five

Liam escorted Grey to the master suite and carried her bag into the closet.

"Does every room in this place get bigger than the last?" she asked on a gasp.

"The living room is bigger than this. After that there's only one bigger, but that's because I ripped out some walls. And it's really more than one room."

"Too confining?"

"I had no need for a mad scientist's lab or the equivalent to a prison cell. Though I did keep certain aspects in place." Like the safe room that would close with the press of a button.

Her throat's pulse bounded. Her eyes popped wide.

Liam never got tired of the jokes he could make about the house. "I told you I got a killer's deal."

"I thought you meant a low price."

"I did, and with it my own personal dungeon."

Grey narrowed her eyes and watched him. He employed every trick he knew to keep a smile off his face.

"You have to be kidding. You're not smiling, but you have to be kidding."

"You should see the toys I put in there. Sinful even by Vegas standards."

That set fire to her cheeks and nearly had him laughing. Rather than push his luck further he changed the subject and mood by stepping close and running a finger along her neck, over the spot where he'd pressed a nibbling kiss. He captured her gaze with his and whispered, "If you run again I'll chase again."

"Liam."

"At least say you'll stay until Ruby is in the clear. Until the danger's passed." The plea cost more than a little of his pride, but every cell in his veins said she was worth it.

The years without Grey had been miserable. The time waiting for her to get to Ruby had been terrifying. One taste of her kiss, though, one touch of her finger to his skin, and he'd seen everything that could be between them.

They didn't speak when she came out after changing. They didn't speak when she crawled beneath the covers he'd turned back. They didn't speak as she'd drifted to sleep with her head cushioned on his pillow.

Hours later, sitting in the chair by a bedroom window, listening to Grey's dainty snore, Liam felt the certainty of what he wanted.

Grey. He wanted Grey.

"No," she whimpered. She twisted and kicked at the covers until they were a tangle below her feet. Pain pinched her voice when she called out again. "No. Don't!"

Liam was up and moving to the far side of the bed. He set his gun on the table and toed off his shoes before easing onto the mattress. Her breath came in pants as she thrashed about. Her short hair spiked against the pillow.

"No. Please." She clutched her throat, clawing at an invisible vice or grip. The flawless skin between her brows flexed in tiny scrunching wrinkles.

"Shh." Each jagged breath was a blade between the ribs. He tried to soothe her as he knee-walked across the giant mattress. The distance wasn't large, but it was too vast.

"Grey. You're safe."

"No!" She screamed and thrashed more violently.

He blocked a foot aimed for his head and then dropped to the mattress. Close enough to touch, he eased a few more inches toward her. As he reached for her he was whispering.

"It's Liam. You're safe." He rested a hand on her arm. She jerked away and raised a knee. He shifted fast enough that the strike missed its mark—barely.

"Grey, it's me, Liam. I won't hurt you." Giving her no time to respond or rebuff his attempts he grabbed her close in one move. Curling her into him and throwing a leg over hers was a risk, but it was necessary. Watching her struggle in fear twisted him into knots tighter than any amount of worry had.

His throat was thick as she trembled in his arms. The police report that had been filed at the time of Jessup's arrest had said he'd killed two pastry shop owners and stabbed a woman while raping her. Liam had assumed, while reading what little he could find since the call from Micah, that Grey had witnessed it all.

Seeing her try to free herself from terror he suspected it was more. He suspected she had instead been a victim, and *that* possibility simply pissed him off. It pissed him off so much he shook more than Grey.

Sometime in the dark hours of morning she relaxed into him. Sometime after that he must have dozed, because he drifted awake to find the sky light enough for him to see Grey's face. His wife's face.

They'd shifted so he was on his back with her curled tight to his side. The stress and fear of her nightmare had eased, leaving the smoothness of peace in their place. The only thing about her that appeared out of control was her hair, and that stood up and out at every angle.

Finger combing it for her, Liam absorbed the simple pleasure of his wife at his side. The night's circumstances sucked, but waking with her in his arms was a dream delivered. Her hair was silky as he smoothed it as much as possible.

"Mmm." Grey stretched against him and his starved body responded.

She slid her hand up his chest and fingered the collar of his shirt. The agent in him was glad he hadn't undressed to watch over her. The husband who'd missed her cursed the barrier, because even if she didn't agree to sex he was missing valuable moments of her skin against his.

"You smell like man," she mumbled against his chest. "I liked that about you."

"You smell like brown sugar, and you taste as sweet," he whispered against her head. "I missed that about you."

Her fingers swept along his collarbone, innocent seduction, and moved along his neck. He rolled his eyes and searched deep for control as the ripples settled beneath the surface and into his veins to heat his blood.

"I had a bad dream." He barely heard her, but he did. He also heard shame, though he didn't understand it.

"I know."

"You made it stop."

"I couldn't watch you suffer."

"I don't dream when you hold me."

Shit. How was a man supposed to respond to that? Smile? Pound his chest and Tarzan yell? Dance a touchdown jig? He settled for a quiet question. "How often do you dream like that?"

"Every night."

Two words shouldn't hold the power to shred him, but her admission, whispered against his chest while her fingers played at his neck, was a shotgun blast of destruction.

She was finished with nightmares. "I'll be here at your side when you close your eyes each night, Grey."

"I want to reject that offer." She shifted and looked up at him. "I really enjoy sleep, though."

Promises sprang to his tongue. Liam bit them back. They were married and though he didn't plan on letting her go again, he couldn't base a life on how they'd started. He would keep his desires and hopes at bay until Grey was ready or willing for more.

He kissed her softly. "Then we'll sleep just like this until everything plays itself out."

"Can it be that simple?"

It's anything but simple. "Yes."

"What about sex?"

He smiled and smoothed her bangs along her forehead. "I'm not going to turn you away. Neither am I going to devour you."

"I don't want to lead you on, Liam. It worries me how tight you're hanging on to our marriage."

"Says the woman still wearing her ring." He shrugged. "Guess my mom's been right all these years."

"How do you mean?"

"I'm a romantic. I leapt with my heart, but do me a favor, Grey?"

"What?"

"Don't worry about me. Focus on you and what you're here to do. Enjoy this house and the safety it provides."

"You make it sound so easy."

"It can be, but you should know one thing."

"What?"

He rolled her to her back and hovered above her. "I really enjoy kissing you."

"You're not an unpleasant kisser."

"I intend to kiss you once a day." He placed a quick peck on the corner of her mouth. "And *that* is not what I consider a kiss."

Her cheeks brightened. Apprehension and anticipation shone in her eyes. Her green eyes.

"Green. My favorite color."

"What?" She blinked, confused. She was easier to read without the shield of contacts in place. He was going to enjoy getting to know her.

"Your eyes. I wondered what color they really were."

"Oh. Right."

Unable to contain his pleasure, he smiled. "You act like you've been someone else so long you've forgotten who you are."

"Sometimes I think I have. Others I'm not sure I'll ever really know."

He considered her claim as he rolled, taking her to the edge of the bed with him. He said nothing as he went into the bathroom. Grey didn't hesitate to follow him in, only she went into the closet where he'd set her bag.

He came out of the water closet to find the shower running, warming up. Grey would run it for five minutes before even testing its temperature. She'd done the same thing in Vegas. Now he wondered if it had more to do with seeking warmth or trying to scrub memories off her skin. He didn't ask, though, from fear of whatever answer she gave if she gave one.

Grey stood at the right side of the double sink brushing her teeth. Liam moved to the left side, his side, and pulled his toothbrush and toothpaste from the drawer.

While he brushed, he moved to the linen closet and pulled out a towel and wash rag for her. She gathered her shampoo and conditioner and a bottle of body wash, took the towels with a nod of thanks and moved toward the shower.

Liam left the room to give her privacy. Standing in the bedroom, he listened to the muted sounds of her undressing, of the shower door opening and closing, and shook his head. They had easily slipped into silence mid-conversation and stepped into a morning routine that felt as natural as if they had been sharing the space for years.

She claimed he was holding too tightly to the idea of them, suggesting she didn't see a future for them, and then she slipped into the space he'd pictured her in.

With his thoughts never straying from the naked woman in his shower, Liam headed downstairs. In the living room, he turned the TV to the morning news. In the kitchen, he started coffee. Instinct said he'd need it more over the coming days than he normally did. And he remembered how much Grey loved the stuff.

After getting set up with a serrated knife and the small butcher block cutting board from the storage slot beneath the island counter top, he retrieved turkey bacon, eggs, cheese and tomatoes from the fridge and then the English muffins from the pantry.

The meal was simple, something he cooked a few times a week, but today the task held more pleasure. He had cooked for company before but never for Grey. It would annoy her if he said anything, but it was sort of like they were stealing time for a honeymoon, if they'd have chosen a honeymoon with a sick sibling and a killer on the hunt.

He cut the tomatoes into thin slices and laughed to himself. Nothing they had done was traditional. With the tomatoes sliced, he turned on the gas beneath the cooktop griddle. While the surface heated, he got a bowl and broke some eggs into it. Fork whipping them until they were fluffy, he skipped the milk most people added to scrambled eggs and instead added lemon pepper for seasoning.

With the bacon spread across the back half of the griddle, he poured the eggs in the middle. As they cooked he forked apart two muffins and laid them along the front.

He was flipping the bacon when Grey walked in. Clearly refreshed from a night's sleep and a shower, the darkness beneath her eyes—blue today—was brighter. Her clothes, more subdued and sensible than the rebellious boldness of the lingerie she'd worn in Vegas, projected confidence. More importantly, they were unimpressive in a way that would allow her to blend into her surroundings.

His wife was smart. She had known she was inviting danger so she had packed disguises. As good as the disguise was, he saw the free spirit beneath the conservative image. Saw it and wanted her out of danger so she could be herself again. And so he could see if she'd kept the sexy scraps beneath.

She closed her eyes and breathed deep. "I smell coffee."

"Sit. I'll get you some." He set the spatula aside and grabbed two mugs from the cabinet. She settled at an island barstool while he filled the mugs and grabbed the creamer from the refrigerator. Her smile when he placed her coffee in front of her fulfilled a fantasy he had entertained since moving in.

"You don't have to wait on me."

"I cook every morning." He played down how much he enjoyed her company, because admitting he would cook just to keep her around, if he thought it would help, would send her running.

"Well thank you."

"Your pleasure is my pleasure."

Grey looked into her coffee. Liam turned back to cooking.

He meant what he said, but he regretted giving the thought voice. If anything would send her running it would be mush. He'd watched his teammates and brother fall beneath love's spell and been humored. He'd seen how soft they acted around their significant others and been haunted.

They'd discovered the kind of connection Liam had seen in his parents. It was the kind of connection that allowed two people to be themselves every minute. They could speak their minds and know the other would understand the intention even if the words were wrong. Laughter was as frequent as yelling, yet with it all was the knowledge that quiet, even silent, moments were natural. The best part of the connection was how it grew deeper and easier every day like one of his mother's hand-stitched quilts growing softer and stronger with use.

Liam craved what his friends and brother had found, but if he didn't learn to shut his mouth on the touchy-feely crap he was going to blow his chance. The resolution to lighten up settled in as he stacked cheesy scrambled eggs, bacon and tomato on a toasted muffin to make open-faced sandwiches.

When he'd sat on the stool beside her, Grey picked up the first of her two sandwiches. "You cook like this every morning?"

He nodded. "There are days I may not eat again until evening or later. I may as well fill up when I can."

She bit into the muffin. Cheese strings followed her retreat from the sandwich. Unpredictably, she did not use her fingers to break the strand. No. She slipped her tongue out and with a quick circle of the muscle she severed the connection.

Muffin suspended before his mouth, Liam stared. She chewed delicately and after she swallowed, the tongue she'd so expertly commanded the cheese with swiped across her lips. His back tightened. How the hell was he supposed to control himself around her when she did things like that?

"This is great," she said before taking another bite.

He nodded and forced his eyes forward. Biting into his own food, he ran crime stats in his head. As distractions went, it was wasted on the power of Grey.

"What did you do before the U.S. Marshals turned you into Grey? What were your hobbies?"

"I tried writing once and quickly learned it was more fun to be a reader." She talked around her food, and as strict as his mom had been that they never speak with food in their mouths, it was cute when Grey did it. Maybe because he never saw her food once it passed her teeth and she didn't sound like she had a mouthful.

"What kind of books?"

"Anything. Romances are fun, but I discovered a few favorites in thrillers. Movies. I *love* movies and watch every one I come across, especially Disney. I can quote many." She'd almost sighed with ecstasy when she talked of movies, and he had no trouble seeing her curled up to watch *Beauty and the Beast*.

Less than conventional. It didn't surprise him. "What else?"

"I'd just dropped out of college and started thinking about applying to the Culinary Institute."

"You wanted to be a chef." She'd been working in a pastry shop that had branched out and begun distributing their muffin and cake mixes to local stores. It made sense she might develop a fondness for it.

She shook her head. "Working in the shop, I had to fill in for the owner's wife one day. She did all the chocolate work and had been showing me a few tips." Nostalgia and sadness slowed Grey's voice. "Both Mr. and Mrs. Matoot were teaching me to cook before..."

"Before Jessup murdered them."

She nodded. "I shouldn't have been there that night. I messed things up."

Feeling responsible for witnessing a death wasn't a normal reaction. Something much worse had happened that night in the pastry shop, and while Liam wanted to question her further, he also wanted to learn about the woman he'd married. He could ask her about Karl Jessup when the team was all together.

"I had a knack for it. Everything I made that day sold twice as fast. A few more test days and the owner's wife moved into the back office to work. I became the amateur chocolatier."

Vibrancy practically bounced to life in her tone and beneath her tinted contacts. Holding back an answering smile was impossible. "You were going to be a chocolatier."

"The Matoots gave me my first taste, then they encouraged me to pursue my talent. I allowed myself to dream." She stopped. Her hand shook beside her plate. "Then I... Then it bubbled and burned."

Her sadness returned as inevitable as grief over losing a loved one. The closest Liam had ever come to real loss was waking alone in Vegas. Grey had known real pain. She'd lost everything—her identity, her sister, her passion, her dream. Then she'd become an admin to an event planner, the one who'd put together the conference he'd attended. She'd walked away from the world of errand running, but her actions had to be limited until they knew she was safe. Safety didn't have to mean she couldn't be indulged.

They finished breakfast in silence, but Liam's mind was chaotic. He would indulge Grey and show her the best of both worlds—safety and passion.

Chapter Six

"Tyler." Liam greeted his friend and teammate with a quad shot venti Americano. "Open up."

Tyler semi-smiled, took the cup and turned it bottom up, essentially pouring it down his throat. After draining the last drop possible he blew a satisfied breath and stretched his neck. "Morning, man."

"I like my morning coffee," Grey chuckled, "but you're smiling like you just orgasmed for the first time in...ever. Which is a really wrong idea since you're in a room with two women you barely know, one of whom is comatose."

"There's no wrong place for that."

"The coffee or the orgasm?" she shot back.

"Pick one." Tyler grinned in a disarming way Grey didn't expect. For that matter she hadn't expected him to look up from his tablet.

"I think I like you." She answered with a grin of her own. It was nice to have reasons to smile and, despite the circumstances, Liam and Tyler were surprisingly fun.

"Just don't like him too much." Liam stepped forward and partially blocked her view of Tyler. Tyler smiled as he turned and moved back to the corner chair.

"Are you saying it's impossible to like multiple men equally? Or that there's something wrong with it?" She rounded Liam and turned her face up to his.

Liam had encouraged her to embrace who she'd been before she was Grey. The trouble there was that pre-Grey fit in even less than Grey. She had been everything he and his friends avoided.

He had also promised she would be accepted as one of the gang as soon as everyone met her. The claim became almost believable when she found herself bantering with Tyler. As Opal she hadn't been the type to keep her opinions to herself. As Grey she needed to melt into the background, though she found that to be a challenge with Liam and his friends. Especially with Liam. "Maybe the idea of being the creamy middle of a Fed sandwich appeals to me."

Liam didn't widen his eyes or narrow them. He didn't frown or scowl. He didn't show any reaction. For seconds he stared, cool as chilled marble. Then he blinked and Grey breathed a sigh of relief she hadn't realized she needed. The momentary delusion of thinking he'd allowed her joke to pass vanished.

A single step, small and determined, closed the distance between them. Liam grabbed her hips and pulled her against him. He was hard, all over, and humming with restraint. The air she'd managed to draw stalled in her lungs.

He'd said he would kiss her once a day. This was it. He was going to kiss her to show her how much she liked him. Or he was out to prove she would never be the middle of a threesome, which was fine. Especially when she allowed herself to remember what being with Liam had been like.

Leaning back, she locked her eyes with his. The hunger she'd seen before was back and it darkened his irises. Or maybe it was the intensity of his body against hers that made her think his eyes darkened. It didn't matter. It only mattered that she was in his arms and he was inches from pressing his lips to hers.

He leaned in, angled toward her ear. She swallowed in anticipation.

"No one else can make you feel like I do, and you know it." He brushed his mouth along her lobe. She shuddered, but he didn't kiss her. "And for your insubordination, you'll have to wait for today's kiss."

Liam looked smug when he set her away from him. Feminine laughter sounded from inside the door. "Ooooh, I knew it. I said the day would come when a woman messed you up. I am so glad it's here."

"What are you doing here, Kieralyn?"

With scowl-hardened lips, Liam turned to the brunette who wore a midnight blue corset-like top and coordinated slacks. Her slipper flats were a pale brown that matched the handbag hanging from her shoulder. A sassy smile painted her lips less subtly than her pink gloss. Uncaring about Liam's much larger size, she bumped him aside and offered a hand. "I'm Kieralyn Cabrera. One of the few women Liam speaks to, and believe me when I say we've all tried to set him up."

"Kieralyn," Liam warned.

Grey accepted the woman's hand, liking her as quickly as she'd liked Tyler. "I'm Greycen Craig, but everyone calls me Grey. And I'm glad he's resisted the hookups. If one had taken I would have missed out on breakfast and coffee this morning."

Kieralyn raised a brow. "Breakfast? Is that what it's called in Vegas?"

"You're getting as bad as Ava," Liam grumbled. "Why are you here?"

"I'm Tyler's relief. And it will look less like Grey's being guarded if I'm with her."

"A girlfriend offering moral support." Grey nodded. She'd left friends in Vegas, but none she would have confided in enough to get support from. Dropping the pretense that her life wasn't perfect eased the tonnage of regret draped her shoulders.

"I'm not a guard. I'm...me." Liam's nose twitched on the last bit. He'd taken care to not say he was her husband and Grey appreciated the effort.

She wouldn't thank him now and get into another round in front of his team, but she could acknowledge him. Still close enough to touch, she rested her fingers on his forearm and waited to speak until his eyes were on hers. "Kieralyn has a point. She's less intimidating."

"If it keeps you out of danger I don't give a damn who I intimidate."

She really didn't want to launch into a debate of any kind with an audience, and she didn't have much time left before her next round of appointments in the living donor process. Equally unwilling to ignore his point, he'd done so much for her already, she took his hand and led him to the bathroom.

Kieralyn was moving closer to Tyler, farther from the bathroom, as Grey closed herself and Liam into the small room. "Liam, don't take this the wrong way, but if Kieralyn's volunteering to go to my appointments I'd like to take her up on the offer."

"Why?" He crossed his arms over his chest. "What's wrong with me?"

"Nothing. I've not found a damn thing wrong with you." She rolled her eyes. "Hell, you even put the toilet seat down."

"Then why do you prefer Kieralyn?"

A large, powerful, confident FBI agent standing in front of her, whining that he wasn't getting his way, was funny and Grey couldn't help it. She laughed. She laughed until her sides hurt and her vision blurred and her bladder bitched. She laughed until she had to cross her legs to keep from peeing her pants. She looked up at Liam, standing with his arms crossed and his scowl hardening more, and she laughed harder.

His scowl deepened. "You just about finished?"

She nodded and tried to control her breathing in an attempt to stop laughing.

"I guess I'm missing the joke."

Under control, she looked up. His stance was still rigid and, God help her, she almost laughed again. "I'm sorry. You sounded so pouty. It's pretty adorable."

"I am *not* adorable."

"You are." She leaned up and kissed his cheek. "And because you are I'll explain myself."

He waved for her to continue.

"Since I walked in that door yesterday, you've been beyond amazing. You've watched out for me here, held me when I dreamed, fed me breakfast and made me laugh." She rested her hands on his crossed arms. Tension vibrated beneath her palms. "When I'm near you I can't think of anything but you."

He raised a brow as if silently saying that wasn't a bad thing. Knowing where he stood on their marriage he probably didn't think it was.

"I need my focus to be on Ruby. I need to be thinking clearly when I meet with these doctors. If I'm thinking about you outside the door or wishing you would hold my hand while they're sticking needles in me, I'm more likely to mess up."

"I would've held your hand if I'd known you didn't like needles."

"I know." Complete seriousness came easily, and with it came honesty. "And that's part of what's tripping me up. So, for the sake of keeping my lies straight, will you please do whatever it is you men do when the women are off somewhere? Let me go to the appointments with Kieralyn."

He drew in a deep breath and released it through his nose. "Fine, but you do what Kieralyn says and don't leave this hospital without me."

"You do realize I got myself into WitSec without you or your team and I made it all the way here from Vegas by myself, right?"

"You're here now and it's not the U.S. Marshals I see offering protection."

"You're right."

He offered his hand. "Do we have a deal?"

"Deal." She slipped her hand in his and since he wouldn't kiss her, she eased up and kissed his cheek. "You really are pretty perfect. It might start to annoy me after a few days."

"Cross me and you'll see the perfection of my anger."

"And then we'll talk about my annoyance level." She dropped back to her heels and smiled. "So, how long have you been dodging these matchmaking attempts?"

"Do you really want the answer?"

"Maybe." *Yes.* She wanted to know if he'd stopped being set up before or after meeting her. Each new thing she learned about him made her more curious. Could he really be as perfect as he seemed?

"Let me know when you decide." Liam opened the door and waited for her to pass before exiting. "She's in your hands, Kieralyn."

A shiver tracked down Grey's spine. If anything went wrong, it would be Kieralyn who felt the perfection of Liam's anger. "Liam."

"She's safe," Kieralyn interrupted Grey. "I'll check in."

He nodded at Kieralyn and then looked at Grey. He retreated into silence again, but she didn't need words to read the worry in his gaze. She'd barely been out of his sight since first seeing him yesterday; he couldn't hide the fear that he wouldn't see her again.

"Go, before you're late for your appointment."

Resistant as she was to a relationship with him, she wanted to reach out and comfort him, to assure him she'd be safe.

"Are you going to kiss her good-bye, Liam?"

He stared at Grey so long she wondered if he might choose now for his kiss of the day. She lifted a foot to step toward him, but he shook his head. "No. We have a deal and good-bye isn't part of it."

Disappointed, Grey turned and left the room with Kieralyn. Two steps down the hall, Kieralyn pounced.

"Okay, give. What's the deal between you and Liam? What hold do you have on him?"

"What do you mean?"

"He's been so uninterested in women for the last few years people in the office are beginning to think he's gay. Then we're sitting around talking about a hit-and-run victim we'd been reading and after one look at her picture in the paper he leaves mid-meal. He's been here or with you since." Kieralyn pressed the elevator's Up button. Grey shook her head and moved to the door for the stairs, remembering Liam's advice.

He'd told Aidan, Tyler and the security guard at his gate they were married. It wasn't exactly a secret, but Kieralyn didn't seem to know. Why hadn't he, or the other two, told her?

Kieralyn was helping protect Grey without knowing why protection was needed. Spilling her guts about everything she did and didn't remember wasn't high on Grey's list of desires, but not telling Kieralyn felt wrong. The woman deserved to know who she was up against.

"Do you have a secret baby hidden away he's not telling us about? Were you his first love who still owns his heart?" Kieralyn and Grey had just reached the first turn in the steps when the door opened again. Looking over her shoulder, she saw the man from the elevator yesterday.

God, so much had happened since yesterday. She tried again to recall where she'd seen him, but her head rejected the attempt. The man still creeped her out so she moved a little faster. She glanced down as they rounded the corner to the next flight of stairs. A shadow fell over him and any hopes of answering Kieralyn evaporated. Pain erupted in Grey's skull as recognition leapt into place.

"I remember the first man I loved." Kieralyn sounded nonchalant, but the questioning look in her eyes when they met Grey's and the way she shifted her hand on her bag left Grey with a different impression. Liam's teammate was on high alert and Grey was grateful she'd taken his advice on the stairs. She could only go up to get away from the man, but at least she could go somewhere.

Kieralyn moved a little closer to Grey's side and continued chatting, probably about a past love, but all Grey heard was the slamming of her blood in her ears. They were in a stairwell with a killer's right-hand man, a man who'd been in the shop at least once, and she couldn't say a word. And because she'd insisted on going with Kieralyn instead of Liam she couldn't hold his hand and feel his warmth.

Grey pushed through the door to their floor before Kieralyn. It closed behind them with a light bang, but the barrier didn't ease Grey's fear. Kieralyn led her down the hall and around the corner, checking behind her a few times.

When they'd rounded the corner and the man had not come onto the floor with them, Grey sagged against the wall for a moment's support. Counting in her head, working to steady her breathing, bile rose. She closed her eyes and pressed a hand to her stomach.

"You okay?" Kieralyn asked. "Do I need to call Liam?"

"I'm fine."

"You're not. Who was the man in the stairwell? Do you know him?"

"I'll be fine." Grey shook her head and reminded herself to breathe. Opening her eyes, she met Kieralyn's. "And yes, we should call Liam."

Kieralyn pulled her phone out. Grey stopped her. "I'll call him. He can get mad at me."

"He's not going to be mad at either of us," Kieralyn argued, but she passed the phone to Grey. It was already ringing.

"Kieralyn." His greeting was terse and more comforting than Grey had imagined possible.

"It's me."

"Grey. What's wrong?"

"Jessup's right-hand man is here. I saw him yesterday but didn't recognize him." She should have recognized him yesterday, but she'd only seen him briefly and her memories of before were, at best, fuzzy. Thinking about him more, her head ached, but she remembered a little more. She'd seen him a few weeks before that last night. She'd been taking the trash out after closing and he'd been standing in the shadows.

Remembering revived some of the memories she only saw pieces of in dreams. Her hands turned to ice and shook. "I don't remember his name. Why can't I remember more?"

Liam cursed. "Where's Kieralyn?"

"Right here. He didn't come onto the floor with us."

"That doesn't mean he won't."

"I know." Her tone sounded harsher than she'd intended. "We're fine. I wanted you to know."

Liam was quiet for several beats. When he spoke it was with more control than she could muster. "Take a few minutes to get composed and then go to your appointment. Kieralyn and I will handle everything else."

"Liam, he has to know I'm me. Why else would he follow me?" Her voice shook as much as her hands. She wanted to help Ruby, but she also wanted to run back into a hole and hide. She wanted to hide so badly it made her feel weak and that made her want to cry.

"Baby, listen to me." Liam spoke quietly, like he had when he'd gathered her into his arms during her nightmare. "You're safe with Kieralyn. She's one of the best."

"Okay."

"Do you trust me to handle this for you?"

"Yes." It was the easiest answer she'd come up with in years. She'd never seen Liam in action. She didn't have to.

"Then trust me. Trust Kieralyn."

"Okay." She exhaled slowly, hugging his assurances close. Her shaking eased.

"And Grey."

"Yeah?"

"If I was with you, I'd kiss you. I'd pull you so close your curves would melt into me and I'd kiss you like I did that night at the top of the Stratosphere Tower."

"That was the night..."

"...we got married," he finished for her.

"That was good." She breathed again, shook a little less. Talking to him, revisiting a beautiful night, soothed her. "That was really good."

"It was. That night...you...are the reason I've dodged every matchmaking attempt. I've only wanted you since."

Grey closed her eyes and continued breathing. Each breath came easier. "You have to have a flaw."

"I have plenty, and you'll be around long enough to find them all."

"I might like that."

"Good. Now go to your appointment and get approved to save your sister's life." He sounded like he was smiling and that made Grey smile. He ended the call with a parting, "Kiss you later."

She was still shaken from seeing Jessup's man but Liam had worked his magic, again, and she was still smiling when she handed the phone to Kieralyn.

"I'm really going to need to know what's between you two," Kieralyn said as they started down the hall again. "Liam's not typically who we look to when someone needs a calming touch."

Grey shrugged and entered the doctor's office. She suddenly didn't mind the idea of Kieralyn knowing she and Liam were married. She much preferred it to dealing with the memories beginning to surface. Hell. She'd rather face the Hulk in a mood to smash.

Chapter Seven

Breck, Aidan, Tyler and Ava had all shown up within fifteen minutes of Liam's call. Tyler had gone straight upstairs to Kieralyn to work on a composite sketch of the man she'd seen. The rest of them had been discussing possible tactics while they sifted through everything Liam had dug up on Karl Jessup. If Grey had spotted his right-hand man, he had to be somewhere.

"Agent Burgess, this hospital room is no place for a strategy session."

"What makes this one different than any of the others?" Liam looked at Nurse Reinhart, who was getting to know them all a little too well. He didn't waste a flattering smile on her, because they both knew she was voicing her protest so she could say she'd warned them. She would only enforce hospital policy if they got in the way of her patient, which they wouldn't do.

"Ms. Donovan is not a member of your team."

"But she's family," he rebutted, "and with us that's the same thing."

Nurse Reinhart shook her head, something his mom did to show her disappointment, but a tiny smile played on her mouth while she jotted notes on Ruby's chart.

"How's she doing?" Liam asked seriously as he stepped away from Ava, Aidan, Tyler and Breck and moved to Ruby's bedside. Grey was still in her consultation with Kieralyn on guard duty outside the door.

"She's getting stronger every day." Nurse Reinhart straightened the sheet covering Ruby's legs and patted her thigh. "The doctors have started to ease her off the coma-inducing meds, so she could wake up in the next day or two. I think hearing you all surrounding her is giving her a reason to fight."

Or hearing her sister's voice had. "Will the kidney transplant be enough?"

"You know we can't know that for sure, but the doctors are hopeful." Nurse Reinhart rested her hand on Liam's arm and squeezed. "It's never good that we have to see you here, but you and your friends have a way of making things brighter while you are. Let me know if you need anything."

Liam glanced at Breck, their team leader, who nodded. They'd discussed whether or not to put some of the staff on notice when Nurse Reinhart had come in. "As a matter of fact, there is something you could do for us. For Ruby."

"Name it."

"We're pretty sure her accident wasn't accidental. And we have reason to believe someone involved in her accident has been seen in the hospital and might try something." Liam walked to the other bed they'd turned into a table and picked up a composite sketch Tyler had worked with Kieralyn on. "Have you seen this man?"

The corner of her left eye scrunched up as she studied the picture. "Not that I recall, but I will keep an eye out. Have you alerted security?"

He shook his head. "The fewer people who know we're looking for him the better. We're not sure what connections he may have."

"You think someone on our staff will warn him."

Liam shrugged. Nurse Reinhart straightened to her full five feet and met his gaze. "I can't let you use our patients as a trap."

"We aren't asking to do that. Just let us know if you see him so we can follow him. We're only looking to minimize a threat that may already be here."

Nurse Reinhart nodded. "I'll keep an eye out."

"Thank you." When the door had closed behind her, Liam turned back to Breck. "I hope you're right about this."

"Tyler's spent all night running the hospital staff. We've dealt with her enough to insert some personal impressions." Breck nodded. "She's the one."

Liam's gut twisted. They'd lined out a plan that ensured three people were on call to help the sisters at any time, even if they had to tag Kami, Ian, Lana, H and Simon. Liam would do whatever it took to make sure Ruby and Grey had enough eyes watching out for them.

"When are you going to tell us why this case, this woman, is so important?" Ava asked.

"Soon." As soon as Grey came back he would let everyone else in on their secret. Questions would be asked and answered because it's what his friends deserved.

"It better be a good explanation," Breck said with his refined quiet. "We're taking a big risk using our resources for a favor. I'll have to justify this to the Bureau."

"It's a risk we've taken before." Ava shrugged.

"More than once," Tyler said with a nod. "This one is just as valid as the others."

Aidan and Tyler shared a grin. Tyler looked back down at his tablet. Aidan cleared his throat. "It's a good one. Though I'll say again it's one I should've known, given that we shared a womb."

"You knew before anyone else," Liam shot back. "Let that be enough."

The door opened. All conversation stopped when Grey and Kieralyn stepped in. Both women looked from Liam to the rest of the team sitting on the edges of the spare bed and the chairs they'd pulled around the bed.

Kieralyn leaned close to Grey. "I think they were talking about you."

Grey slid her gaze to Kieralyn and chuckled. "I think that's what they call an understatement."

Liam moved to Grey and turning his back on everyone in the room met her gaze. "You okay?"

"Yes." She nodded to the group in the room. "Though I'm pretty sure you're about to test that theory."

Liam moved so he stood behind her with his hands on her shoulders. "Grey, you've met my brother Aidan, Tyler, who is our tech God, Kieralyn, with charms even the NSA couldn't resist."

"Well," Kieralyn said with a wink, "one NSA guy in particular. Unless we want to also count Dante."

Liam continued. "Breck is our team lead, and Ava is the colorful one of us, her past that is."

"Spy, killer, call-girl, empath, FBI agent." The dark-haired beauty shrugged. "I'm the complete package."

Grey lifted a hand in a wave. Liam pressed his thumbs lightly into the back of her shoulders. "This is Grey. My wife. She's been in WitSec until her sister, Ruby, was hospitalized. Now she's back, without U.S. Marshal protection, and we're pretty sure the man she's supposed to testify against knows."

"Jessup." Breck nodded.

Grey's shoulders rose and fell in a sigh. Liam imagined she was frowning, but his way was the most expedient. Everyone needed to know what they were getting into. Breck needed to know why they should take on the case. He'd given them all the necessary answers quickly.

"Why didn't you tell us?" Ava asked.

He could spell it out so many different ways, but didn't want any blowback landing on Grey. "She didn't think it would be right to ask me to go into protection with her."

"And you couldn't risk coming into our world," Kieralyn addressed Grey directly.

Grey shook her head in answer to Kieralyn.

Aidan crossed the room and stood before Grey. With a smile, he pulled her away from Liam and hugged her close. "Welcome to the family, sis."

When Aidan released her, Tyler was there for a hug. Then Breck and Ava and finally Kieralyn. They each welcomed her, and with every hug the tightness Liam hadn't noticed released from around his heart. He'd known they would step in and help her, but their automatic acceptance of her meant more to him than he'd thought it could.

When Kieralyn released Grey, she passed her back to Liam. He ran a hand along Grey's arm. "Sorry I didn't warn you."

"I've lived with enough lies. It's fine."

His sisters had always been supremely pissed when claiming things were *fine*. Grey's tone didn't hold the same edge, but neither was she pleased. He would have to think about that later, though, because he wasn't inviting an argument in front of the team. "They had to know."

"And they couldn't know part without knowing all." She nodded. "I figured that out in the stairwell with Kieralyn."

Tyler got down to business. He led Grey to the corner chair and placed his tablet in her lap. He tapped the screen a few times and called up a gallery of images. "Tell me if any of these men look familiar. To enlarge…"

He trailed off when she double tapped the screen and then began flipping through the images with a flick of her finger. "I took the description Kieralyn gave me and ran it against known associates of Jessup."

"I didn't see his men often, only once that I remember, but he gives off a kind of eeriness that's memorable. And from what I heard, he was entirely devoted to Jessup."

Tyler left her to her search and talked with the team. "The warden says Jessup's maxing out his Internet time each week, and he's had an increase in people trying to visit."

"He's running his business from inside," Breck stated, "and damn if it doesn't sound like he's planning something."

"We need to know what, though."

"That's easy," Grey said from where she scanned images. "I'm the only thing keeping him in prison. He wants me dead."

"Well that's not happening."

Liam looked over to Grey, who was still flipping through pictures. It wasn't enough that she told them whom she'd seen. She needed to ID him visibly without any prompting. They needed evidence. "Marshal Carpenter said their entire case hinged on her testimony."

"Who?" Breck asked.

"The U.S. Marshal assigned to Grey until she left the program. When she left Vegas to come here he called."

"Why?"

Liam watched Grey, measuring her reaction to his answers. "When I ran her name a few years ago I triggered their system. He thought we'd been looking into Jessup so he gave me a head's up. He didn't seem to know we're married."

"Why'd you run her name?" Aidan asked.

"Because she left him as fast as she married him."

Liam's gaze snapped to Ava. As an empath she was good at reading people, but not their minds. Grey spoke before he could.

"I didn't know he was a Fed when I married him. I saw his badge and Miami address and freaked."

"Because you and Jessup are from here," Liam said.

"I never mentioned you to Micah. To anyone."

Grey nodded and thankfully that seemed to be the end of the questions about their history.

"So this is all a trap," Breck stated. "Is that the theory we're working on?"

"Yes," Grey answered without looking up from the tablet. "At least it's Micah's."

"And if he's not helping Jessup, the man we saw could be vying for position of top dog," Kieralyn tacked on. "And he'd need Grey out of the way as much as Jessup."

"Because he can't know she won't name him during the trial," Ava finished.

Tyler pulled out a second tablet, and set his fingers to work. "I read most of the file the Bureau has on Jessup—it's a big one filled with circumstantial evidence. I've sent a request to the other agencies to see if they have anything."

"Is there anything we can use that we haven't already discussed?" Aidan asked.

Tyler shook his head. "Not that I've found. We need to focus on identifying the players and keeping these women safe so Grey can be at the trial."

Grey approached them and laid the tablet on the bed by Tyler with the full gallery showing. "Fifteen is the man I saw in the elevator and stairwell. If he's not in charge, then number twenty-two would be my guess. I saw him more frequently. Number seven is also vaguely familiar. Maybe he ran a delivery or two at the shop."

"Delivery?" Breck asked.

"Drugs." Grey stuck her hands in her pockets and stood rigidly near Tyler. "They had a whole system worked out with the Matoots. I got in the way."

Tyler took the tablet and after a few taps had no doubt initiated detailed searches into the men she'd identified.

Liam leaned against the wall, struggling with the boundaries he had to obey now that the team was looking into the case. He'd seen the lingering damage of whatever she'd seen, and he didn't want to ask about it, but they needed to know and she'd have to talk about it at trial. "What did you witness, Grey? How often did you come across Jessup? Can you explain their system?"

She turned to him but didn't meet his gaze. "I told you about learning to work with chocolate in the pastry shop."

"Yes."

"Before that I mixed the batters for our products. Sometimes I helped package stuff for the retail outlets we sold to."

"And Jessup?"

"The owners introduced him as a customer. We had several local stores that sold our mixes. He looked and acted the part, and all the men who did pickups for him wore the same uniform. There was no reason to doubt the story."

"What changed?" Liam prompted.

"Everything we made for Jessup was for a standing order. Turns out he was the dealer and his product was hidden in the packaged mixes. An employee took one of the mixes and a kid died from an overdose. When the cops started looking at the Matoots they contacted Jessup and demanded he find another way to move his merchandise."

She rolled her shoulders, rubbed her neck. Liam's palms itched to comfort her, but he resisted. She needed to know she was strong enough to get through the retelling, because that would help her move past anything else she faced.

"I had gone back to clock out after making a delivery, and I walked in to see Jessup holding a gun to Mrs. Matoot's head. He demanded that Mr. Matoot change his mind, that he agree to continue distributing. Mr. Matoot refused so Jessup pulled the trigger. He gave Mr. Matoot another chance to comply. Instead, he fell to Mrs. Matoot's side and refused again. Jessup shot him the same way."

She spoke mechanically, as if she was divorcing herself from what had happened. If she could maintain that, it would help her stay calm on the witness stand when the day came. "From what I heard, the weapon hasn't been recovered so there's nothing to tie him to the murders. All the orders were verbal, payments were made in cash. There was no record of a store receiving those deliveries."

She didn't mention the part about the woman being stabbed and raped. The evasion made Liam more certain she was the woman.

Breck ended her retelling by standing and doling out tasks. "Tyler will do what Tyler does, running the men Grey identified.

If there's a paper trail he'll find it. Aidan, do you mind talking to Lana?"

Aidan scoffed. "Yes, but it won't matter. This is the kind of story she's most attracted to. If I bring her in I can at least convince her to hold off before writing anything."

Aidan's willingness to talk about work with his journalist fiancée was becoming more commonplace, but it was strange. The only thing that made it seem normal was knowing they still argued at every turn about how cases and stories should be handled.

"Ava, could you reach out to Simon? He's good at finding information people don't want found. Maybe he can help."

"He's watching Ruby tonight, but I'll call him. Then I need to follow some leads on a few other cases."

Breck nodded. Simon was a private investigator who'd tracked down and then kept hidden some of the best-hidden people and then he'd tracked others through those connections. He'd also, unexpectedly, become close friends with Ava's fiancé, H.

"Kieralyn and Liam, you two keep an eye on Grey and Ruby. Liam, I'll cover you on the cases you've been working. And I'll talk to the director."

Breck, Aidan, Ava and Tyler gathered their things and with a final round of welcomes and assurances for Grey said good-bye. Grey stopped Tyler when he placed a hand of support on her shoulder.

"Tyler, you're already doing so much, but could I ask another favor?"

"Name it."

She looked at her sister, licked her lips and asked, "Would you look into Ruby? I'm curious what her life's been like. If she had anyone we should find a way to contact."

He flicked a glance at Liam before looking back to her. "We've already started. I'll make sure to send Liam the latest information."

"Have you found anyone?"

Tyler shook his head. "It appears as if she's kept to herself the last several years. She works from home and aside from the grocery store she rarely goes out."

"So she's been alone."

Sorrow pinched Liam's heart at the guilt in Grey's voice. Tyler didn't tell her she'd made the right choice, that she'd kept Ruby and herself safe for five years. Kieralyn and Liam also remained silent, because they couldn't really know she'd made the right choice. They could only hope for the best.

Tyler nodded and made his exit, leaving Liam alone with Grey, Kieralyn and Ruby. Liam wanted to pace, to run, to pound his fist into someone until they were bloody and bruised. He wanted to release every ounce of hindering helplessness. But he needed to be steady for Grey, so he suppressed his wants and focused on the next step.

Grey walked to Ruby's bed and lifted her sister's hand. She sat on the side of the bed, cradling Ruby's hand in her lap. Her shoulders shook as she leaned forward and laid her head on Ruby.

"I'm sorry I left you," she whispered to her sister, "but I'm here now."

Liam swallowed the urge to go to Grey. Instead, he nodded for Kieralyn to follow him. Stepping into the hall, he left Grey to confront her guilt in privacy. When they got home, though, he would pull her close and find a way to begin putting her heart back together.

Chapter Eight

The ocean was about ten minutes away from Liam's home, but its breezy scent reached clean and heady through the car's open windows. Grey had asked about driving her own car, but Liam insisted on taking his, which left her little to do except watch him and the passing scenery.

She inhaled, pulling the peace of the ocean's scent deep into her—muscle, cell, bone. She'd missed the smell and the crash of the waves. Times like these she would have visited her favorite sandy haven to clear her head. Now, a visit was out of the question, since she had to avoid her favorite spot.

Unlike the night before, when Liam neared the security gate to his division, the guard opened the gate automatically. Liam waved and drove toward the house.

"Your team is pretty impressive," she said in an effort to fill the annoying silence.

"We've been through a lot together." He rubbed the top of his fingers along hers. He'd been touching her with the same soft gestures all day and each time he did her skin popped with goose bumps. He'd said nothing, but every gesture suggested intimacy, which made her crave him while reminding her why they'd never last.

"Which could tear you apart."

"Except it made us stronger. We're good on our own, but together we're unbeatable."

She understood the theory even if it wasn't one she could say she'd ever witnessed. His claims about how wonderful his friends were had been confirmed with every hug she'd been welcomed by. And each hug had twisted painfully, because she would leave Liam. Now, that meant she would also leave his friends.

"I know they can take some getting used to. Mainly how much we're in each other's lives, but you'll get used to them."

"Liam." She pulled her hand from beneath his and placed it in her lap. "I need to tell you something."

He pressed the button for the garage door. "You can tell me anything."

"I'm..." Her words fell away as the door rose. The convertible had been moved into the far spot and her dented up Corolla with its stained interior and two-hundred-and-fifty-thousand mile wear and tear sat in the spot beside Liam's.

The heap couldn't be more out of place.

Like her.

"You're what?"

"What's my car doing here?" She'd assumed it would sit in the hospital lot when he insisted he drive.

"We couldn't leave it in the lot. For all we know Jessup's people would find it and tamper with it."

"So you had it brought here."

It was sound logic. Everything Liam did for the sake of her safety was based on sound logic. The quality was equal parts endearing and frustrating. His latest gesture of getting her car, ten years past its expiration date, to his house turned a spotlight on their differences.

He was uptown. She was ghetto in a fading mask.

Logic and focus drove him. Spontaneity and guilt drove her.

He eased to a stop by her beater and put his machine in Park. "Where would you have rather seen it?"

"An impound lot. The bottom of the ocean. In a scrap pile." She waved at the eyesore that had barely survived the trip from Vegas. "I'd rather see it anywhere but here."

Liam studied her, long and serious. His silence wasn't awkward, but neither was it easy. It was telling, as if he saw into her and could pull every insecurity to the surface with the lightest tug.

"You don't think you belong here."

"I know I don't."

"You think my friends and my house are more than you deserve. Even for a short time."

She flinched. They were so much better than her, but the only way to make him understand would be to tell him everything. He would never know everything. She would never look into his eyes and see disgust looking back at her.

"You intend to leave, Grey." The stark acceptance in his tone stabbed at her. "I intend to make that very difficult."

"Why?" Her voice cracked. "Why do you want me here?"

"I'm not sure you'd believe me if I told you, so when you're ready to stay, if you get ready, I'll answer that question."

"Your answer may be what I need to change my mind." It wasn't, but the idea that it could be held appeal.

He brought her hand up and placed a kiss on her wrist. "You have to want it for your own reasons."

"Why can't you make things easy?"

He was smiling as he leaned across her to open her door. His arm brushed her breast and a new round of goose bumps sprang to life. "The best things in life come with a little pain and heartbreak."

"And how do you define 'best things'?"

He kissed her cheek and kept his response to himself as he got out of the car and headed inside. Grey sat for a minute, stared at his retreating back and then the closed door as hollowness flooded her stomach.

Since their reunion he'd opened every door for her and showered her with affection. She'd wanted him to ease up, to stop so she could think straight. He had and she found herself facing something that felt suspiciously like sadness. It weighed heavy in her heart and sat thick in her throat. His departure left her feeling...empty.

Unsure what she'd say when she caught up to him she followed. Reconciliation with why she felt the way she did was far off, yet when she opened the door to the kitchen it became unattainable.

"Of course I'm happy to see you. I only asked what you were doing here." Liam held a sprite of a woman in his arms and hugged her close.

Dark hair and alabaster skin, with a frame so petite she looked fragile enough to crack beneath Liam's large hands, the other woman had her legs around his waist and her arms around his neck. "I'm in town for a conference. You said the place was always open."

Nice. He'd acted like he'd only been interested in Grey, yet he'd given his key and security code to someone else.

The woman, who even sounded like Liam, raised her head and smiled at Grey as she tapped Liam's shoulder. "Hi."

He set her down. Despite her three-inch heels she barely reached his chest. She looked like a child. Rather, she had the face of a child and the body of a siren.

Grey did not return the child woman's greeting. She was too busy wrestling down the sadness that had quickly morphed and boiled toward rage. Or it could be jealousy.

"Grey, come meet Gara, one of my all-time favorite people."

She didn't want to meet Gara, or any other woman making herself welcome in his house. Considering Grey'd be leaving in a couple of weeks, however, she had no right to say anything. Spine stiff, stomach churning with dislike, she nodded a greeting.

The girl didn't look *as* young a little closer, but she still couldn't be more than twenty-one. "Hello."

The right corner of Liam's top lip twitched with an unrealized smile. He was laughing at her. There was some joke only he was privy to and his resulting humor made her the butt. In her eyes that made him an ass.

"Gara." He stepped around the other woman and took Grey's hand. "Sis, this is Grey."

Sis.

"You..." His sister's mouth dropped. Knowing her name didn't make Grey want to use it. Using it only stood to make her personable and *that* would *not* do.

Gara's gaze darted between Liam and Grey. "I'm not sure what question to start with."

Liam placed his palm at the small of Grey's back. "She's my wife."

"Your... You... Oh my God!" Gara squeed at an eardrum-shattering pitch. "When? Does Aidan know? Have you phoned home?"

She squeed again and hand-flapped her way to Liam. Grey sidestepped. Gara grabbed Liam into a hug, bouncing. Then she released Liam and turned on Grey.

Excitement shone in the eyes so like Liam's as she stepped forward. Grey stepped back with her hands raised in defense. She hadn't just come face-to-face with a lover. This was worse.

She'd just met more of his family and this family wasn't the calm sort from earlier. No. This family was the high-strung, impressionable sort Grey shouldn't be allowed near.

Grey's lungs wouldn't work right. She couldn't get air. Her head buzzed. The muscles along her spine tightened, fisting around each vertebra.

"I'm gonna...go..." She pointed toward the back door as she moved away. "Air."

She couldn't move fast enough to get away from Liam and Gara. The introduction to his team hadn't been easy, but it hadn't been horrible. They were helping protect Ruby. Aside from Aidan they weren't family. And they'd been in the hospital, which was far less personal than Liam's home.

Meeting his sister, who wanted to make sure his parents were notified, spelled doom. Meeting his family, the family Liam had said would be Grey's, the family Aidan had welcomed her into, was the last thing she wanted to be dealing with.

Facing Jessup again in that storage closet held more appeal.

The walls moved in, pressing closer. Closer.

"Grey! Wait!"

She ignored Liam's call and escaped into the backyard. Lush and stunning with a zero edge pool and amazing landscaping it held no soothing powers of seclusion. The trees bordering the property seemed promising. She headed for them and kept going until she found the seclusion she'd sought.

The neighborhood's natural foliage of giant trees dripping with moss and the soft ground that gave beneath her feet were almost as good as the beach she'd have once visited. Her chest ached as she sank down.

Running hadn't always been an option, but she'd gotten used to it, gotten used to being ready to run even if she didn't. Running again because she felt trapped ripped the scabs off barely covered wounds.

Humidity clung to her cold, shaking hands. Sweat dripped from her brow, but she couldn't get warm. And she couldn't shake the memories sticking to her tighter than her shadow.

Drawing her knees to her chest, hugging herself with her head down, she begged for merciful relief. It didn't come. Only the memory came.

The shop's lights were turned off, but the Matoots never left less than three hours after closing. It didn't matter how clean the staff left the place or how perfectly they balanced the till, the couple went over it again.

Or so they always explained.

In the backroom, the Matoots were dealing with bags of cake and muffin mixes. Or she'd thought that's what they were doing. The labels were identical to the others, with the exception of the font.

On the stainless-steel counter sat clear, tightly sealed bags of pills stamped with a one-eared rabbit. Beside the counter was a giant container of dry mix, but instead of filling the bags with the mix they were dumping them out. The pile of pill bags grew with each one.

Opal's—she hadn't been Grey yet—fingers shook at the sight of the latest rage on the streets. White Rabbit was the latest brand of ecstasy everyone was wanting.

Her failure to resist it had already caused too much trouble, so she found herself struggling between stepping forward, not sure what she'd say, and retreating. To her left the back door opened, deciding for her. She darted silently into the storeroom and watched from the small window. She wouldn't confront the Matoots, but if she could sneak just one pill...

Karl Jessup came in, but he wasn't dressed like usual. Instead of khaki Dockers and a polo he wore a slick-looking suit and gold watch.

"I'm hearing things," he said in the slow drawl of the South. "Things I don't like."

Mr. Matoot, wiry thin with his fifty plus years showing in the gray hairs covering his head, turned to Jessup. He wasted no time getting to the point. "We can't take these risks any longer."

"We had a deal," Jessup pointed out with a daring lift to his eyebrow. His charm suddenly seemed dangerous. "I help you get your daughter into the country, and you distribute cake mixes."

"A boy's dead because he got his hands on one of these bags," Mrs. Matoot cried as she dropped another bag of pills onto the pile.

"A mistake that cut into my profits, but I let whoever made it live."

"If your drugs hadn't been here the incident wouldn't have happened. Now we have cops sniffing around because they found a pill in the bag. We can't do this anymore."

"I see." Jessup sounded calm as he reached beneath his suit jacket.

A chill wrapped around Opal's shoulders. It had nothing to do with the cooler temperature of the closet.

"Let me simplify things for you. You'll continue keeping your part of the deal and get rid of the cops." He pulled a gun and pressed it to Mrs. Matoot's temple.

Opal's pulse points—every one in her body—slammed against the restriction of her skin.

"Or, I will give them something to sniff."

Mr. Matoot shook his head. "We don't trust you. Our girl should be here by now."

"You think I don't keep my word?"

Mr. Matoot notched his chin higher and stepped closer to his wife. "No."

Jessup shrugged and pulled the trigger. Opal flinched. Mrs. Matoot fell. Her blood seeped onto the lavender tile. Mr. Matoot didn't seem to notice as he went to his knee at his wife's side. Vomit rolled up Opal's throat. She swallowed it and a scream when Jessup swung the gun and aimed at Mr. Matoot.

"Do you doubt me now?"

"No." Tears streamed down Mr. Matoot's cheeks as he looked at his wife, stroking her cheeks. Loss and sadness didn't weigh on his tone, though. Decisiveness did. "I think you got our daughter here long ago, and I wouldn't be surprised if you killed her to keep us in line."

"I guess I'm out of leverage." Jessup pulled the trigger a second time. Mr. Matoot collapsed onto Mrs. Matoot's chest. He was still moving when Jessup bent over with his hands braced on his knees. "Your daughter is here. She's been staying with me."

He pulled the trigger again. Opal failed to stop the new surge of vomit, but she managed to grab an empty bucket.

Wiping her mouth with a cleaning rag, hating herself as much as she feared Jessup, she looked through the window again. Jessup was on the phone ordering someone to get their ass in gear. Then he hung up and began pulling bags of drugs out of large bags of powdered sugar that sat nearby.

He'd blackmailed and killed. Now he was cleaning up the evidence. She needed to call the police, but her phone was out front and there was no way she'd try to sneak past Jessup. She would stay hidden and wait him out. That seemed safer.

Then he looked toward the door she hid behind. She ducked and looked for cover in case he'd seen her. There was no cover, but there were several more bags of the powdered sugar.

Her heart sprinted when her legs couldn't.

The knob turned. The door opened. Light glinted off the blade of a kitchen knife.

She should have made a run for it.

A firm hand came down on her shoulder. She screamed, grabbed at her offender and rolled, flipping him over her head. She'd scrambled several feet and stood before his voice registered. Her name.

"Grey. It's me. Liam." He stood but instead of approaching her he remained still and raised his hands. "I'm not going to hurt you."

Her breaths came in sawing gasps that burned, though each one returned a little more normalcy.

The storeroom and kitchen made way for grass and trees. The cool air in the closet became a humid breeze that failed to warm her skin or blood.

"I'm here, Grey." Liam's Scottish brogue deepened as he moved close and rubbed soothing circles between her shoulder blades. The gliding rhythm of his hand against her shirt was warm, and its warmth reached into her heart and eased the frenetic pace. Breathing easier, she leaned into his touch.

"I'm not going to let anyone hurt you." Guiding her with the lightest pressure of his fingertips, he turned her in his arms and held her close. "I'd rather you not come out here alone again."

She felt safe with him touching her. She wanted to feel safe alone. "I can't do this, Liam."

She pushed away from him and stiffened her resolve along with her spine. "I can't stay in your house and meet your family and pretend to be happily married and rely on you to keep the nightmare away at night and act like everything's going to be okay."

Her voice pinched at the higher octave, but she couldn't stop. "Your sister is barely an adult, and I can't be anywhere near her. It's too dangerous. I'm not fit. I won't find out what Jessup's people might do to her if they thought it would get to me. She's not going to be victimized because of me."

"She's in her mid-twenties and she isn't staying here, so there's no danger to her. Her cab should be here any minute."

"You said it earlier, Liam." Grey went on without stopping or caring that Gara was leaving. "I intend to leave. I was going to wait, play this out, but I've changed my mind." She walked backward toward the house, shaking her head as she went. "I appreciate your efforts to help, but I'm leaving. Now. Don't try to stop me."

"Grey."

"No, Liam. Your logic's not going to work this time. I'll be careful, but I'm going to suffocate if I stay in your house and hear the word 'wife' out of your mouth one more time."

"Then I won't say it."

"You'll be thinking it and that's just as bad." He could catch her easily, but she still turned and ran for the house. In the kitchen, she slammed the back door and kept going until she'd reached the bedroom closet where her bag was. After throwing the few things inside she'd pulled out, she zipped the lid closed and headed downstairs.

She made it to the garage and then to her car without seeing Liam or Gara. Her key was in the ignition and the garage door was open. Grateful not to have to fight him, she tossed the bag in the passenger seat and got behind the wheel.

Twisting the key, listening to the weak engine cough to life, she looked toward the kitchen door. He was letting her go. The freedom should thrill her, but, instead, she felt like the too-stupid-to-live horror-movie heroine who'd just run outside to check a sound.

The nightmare was coming. She may as well find her Elm Street.

Chapter Nine

Liam had changed a lot about the home Madame X had used to house her call girls. One thing he'd kept was her security system, well, except that he'd pulled the cameras out of the bathrooms and redirected the ones in the bedrooms so they were on the windows and doors only.

Standing in the control room inside the safe room, he watched Grey head through the house and braced himself against the agony of loneliness. He'd sent his baby sister to Aidan's, fairly certain she'd call their parents with the news that should come from him, and had gone to be with Grey, to deal with whatever had scared her away. Instead of staying, she'd called it quits.

Waking alone in Vegas hurt less than watching her walk away. Hell, she hadn't walked. She'd run. The house had never seemed so empty and he'd have sworn it creaked with sadness the farther away she pulled.

Unwilling to mourn the absence of his bride—a state of life he should view as normal—Liam flipped off the monitors he'd watched her on. Grabbing his tablet, Bluetooth and determination, he headed for the door. She'd wanted freedom, and as far as she knew he'd given it to her.

Tyler wasn't the only one capable of using tech, and Aidan wasn't the only one of them who had trust issues when it came to a woman. Certain Grey would make a break for it sooner or later, Liam had bugged her car and phone with a tracker. Taking it a step further, he'd bugged her with a little device Ian, the NSA's expert listener and Kieralyn's husband, had created a few years earlier.

The hair-thin tracker with listening capabilities could be stuck to a person's skin or clothes with an adhesive spray. For up to a week the tagged person could be surveilled without knowing, and if the bug came off they would simply think they'd found a gray hair.

Liam had meant it when he said Grey wasn't getting away again. A few thumb swipes and taps on his tablet proved his point as the green dot that was now Grey blipped to life on the map. His phone connected automatically to the Bluetooth in his car when he pushed the power button. He snapped the tablet into a dash dock.

His phone rang as he was backing out of the garage. "This is Burgess," he answered.

"Mr. Burgess, sorry to bother you, but your wife is saying she's leaving."

Liam smiled at the idea of what must be going through Grey's head when Mr. Lambert wouldn't allow her to automatically pass. She had to know that a word from Liam would stop her, giving her no recourse. She didn't know that while Liam wanted to stop her, he would listen to the advice his mother had given him many times as a teen.

If you want a girl to be yours, give her freedom. If it's meant to be she'll be back.

Letting Grey go, didn't mean losing sight of her. He was curious what she would do on her own. "She's safe. Let her go."

"Yes, sir. Have a good evening."

"Thank you." Liam disconnected the call and watched the dot on his display move onto the main road as he neared the division's entrance.

Mr. Lambert shook his head as Liam drove past with a wave. He'd had enough chats with the man to know he'd expected to see a pursuit. Fortunately, Grey didn't know him so well.

Liam called Tyler as he drove.

"You so bored with married life you need to call me?" Tyler joked.

"I could go for some boredom right now."

"Me too. Someone's trying to hack my firewalls. What's up?" Tyler brushed it aside that his system was being messed with, but the brush off was only verbal. He'd take the attack personally and work around the clock until he found the hacker.

A few miles ahead of him, Grey took an exit and made some immediate maneuvers, looping back, before getting back onto the highway. She did the same thing every few exits, each time giving Liam time to catch up. He wasn't sure if she thought she was being followed or if she was being cautious, though he hoped it was the latter.

"Has there been any movement toward Ruby?" Liam asked.

"None that Simon has reported."

"Can we use any of your cameras?"

"You want to clear the path?"

"I don't love the idea, but I want to see them safe."

"You run it by Breck?"

For Tyler, the man who'd joined the FBI after hacking them, to have an issue with pushing the limits they were getting close to a big line. "I'd rather him have deniability."

"Aidan too?"

"Yes." Especially Aidan. Director Quinn would expect perfection from his son-in-law-to-be.

Tyler held his thoughts for several minutes. He couldn't be pushed into breaking the rules, at least not before he considered the consequences. Finally he asked, "Why are you asking for this?"

"I want Grey safe."

Her green marker on his tablet made a few more back tracks. She was doing more than even he did for precaution's sake. His heart sped. He accelerated.

"Some reason she's not safe with you?"

Truth tasted oddly like crow. "She's not with me."

"Shit! How the hell did that happen?"

"Gara showed up. Grey freaked and said she was putting too many people at risk."

"She's worried about your family. That's nice."

"Except she's family too."

"She's not seeing it that way."

"Well she needs to, damn it!"

"You're not going to win that argument with demands." Tyler applied a data-like logic to the moment. "Or by changing the plan. For now all we need to do is keep things calm and watch the sisters closely."

"When did you become the logical one?"

"When you fell in love," Tyler rebutted, but they both knew Tyler had always been the logical one. "Are you tracking Grey?"

"Yes. She's heading toward the beach."

"Call her. Ask if she's found a place to stay and remind her not to use plastic. And Liam?"

"Yeah?"

"If you want her to completely trust you, back off a little. Call in Kami or Lana if you need to, but give Grey some space."

The side of Liam's nose was twitching as he hung up and called Grey. She didn't answer so he left a voicemail with Tyler's advice. And though he doubted it would do any good, he ended with, "Come back to the house. Gara left. You'll be safe."

The same pain that had stabbed him when she'd walked away returned. Dread drove him closer to recklessness. Grey's green marker stopped at a motel near the beach.

When he caught up and parked in a lot across the street, he activated the wire on her neck. She mumbled each room number she passed, which told him which ground floor room she was in. Beach access on the back gave her two exits. Smart. He just hoped she'd listened to him about the credit card. If not, Jessup's men, if they were around, and he had to believe they were, could easily find her.

His phone rang. "Aidan."

"You have that huge house and are on record saying family would never be in the way there." Not Aidan. Lana. Worse, it was Lana launching into a tirade before he could explain. "So why is your baby sister here instead of somewhere in that massive home of yours?"

"Grey left because of Gara."

"Then she's not the right woman for you."

"She doesn't want the danger following her to blow back on the wrong people. On my family."

"Awwww. She sounds sweet."

So sweet she kept leaving him. "So now you know why Gara is there. Share Aidan's rare turn to host or go to your own apartment, but I have more pressing problems."

"Your wife is throwing you off your game, Liam. You're normally the more easygoing one."

"And Aidan has issues with reporters. We all have our buttons."

"And you're Grey's. She's just not ready to admit it."

He laughed at how quickly Lana changed her opinion of the woman she had yet to meet. This was one case when Lana was wrong. Grey's only weakness was Ruby.

"Are you finished yelling at me?"

"I never yell, and yes. But before you hang up..."

He waited.

"I did some digging and I'm pretty sure Grey was more than a witness to Jessup's crimes. I think she was also a victim."

"Me too." And she was in the motel alone where he couldn't hold her if the dream came again.

"There's also a rumor Jessup's hired a hitter. Aidan's checking known possibilities to see if anyone's moving in the area."

"Son of a bitch."

"Stay safe," Lana said before hanging up.

Unable to sit while anxiety built and built, Liam got the duffel out of his trunk and used the backseat to change into running clothes. Changed, he pulled the custom backpack he'd had made for runs from the bag. A traditional zipper pouch allowed him to stow his tablet and keys, but outside access pockets with Velcro fasteners held his weapon, cuffs, cell and badge.

With his Bluetooth headset activated so he could hear Grey through the listening app on his tablet, he scanned what he could see of the front of the motel between the trees. Everything looked normal, if having a state's witness hiding in one of the rooms was normal. He headed toward the beach where he used the practice of stretching to scan the area.

The sun was setting so the tourist crowds were clearing, making room for the locals and couples indulging in evening walks. The motel rooms had all the blinds or double glass doors open to allow the sun and scent of the ocean in. All but one. Grey had her doors closed and the vertical blinds slatted so they were closed enough to allow some light in, but not allow people to see in.

She was being cautious, but he'd still rather have her at his side.

Jogging toward the sunset, he scanned the faces on the beach and listened to Grey move around in her room. She ordered a pizza and then flipped on the television. Leonard and Sheldon from *The Big Bang Theory* argued about their roommate agreement. Liam chuckled as he ran, but not Grey.

Grey made no sound, which aroused his curiosity. Sweat poured off him, but it had more to do with anxiety racing through his blood than from the running. He'd turned back up the beach, keeping the motel within sight the whole time, when a knock sounded on her door.

"Who is it?"

"Pizza."

There was a metallic snap, a wallet, then the rustle of some bills before the lock was turned back. Fear coiled in Liam's gut. He needed to *see* her, not just hear her. He needed to know she was safe. To know that the pizza guy really was a pizza guy.

His pulse slammed as he ran harder to get back. He shouldn't have gone as far as he had.

His head cleared of emotional distractions in time to hear Grey tell the guy to have a good night before closing and locking the door.

Liam eased his speed to a walk. They may be married, but he barely knew Grey. A certificate that named her as his wife wasn't reason enough to crave her like he did. He couldn't pinpoint the how or why but he felt whole when she was with him. His life didn't suck without her, but with her it was definitely better.

He reached the starting point of his run and considered continuing, but a man on the beach caught his attention.

Wearing black suit pants and loafers with a tight black shirt tucked in, he sat on the sand. His legs were bent up with his biceps resting on his knees. Dark aviator glasses obscured his face. He might look like a man decompressing from a long day if he faced the water.

He faced Grey's motel, though.

Liam took a few steps toward the man, not sure what he'd say. He wasn't one of the men Grey had identified as Jessup's, but Lana said there could be a hitter in play. He could be a new hire, or someone she hadn't seen before, or someone who'd recognized her from her old life, or just a guy on the beach looking for a thrill.

He could have followed her from the subdivision if he was good enough. Or a tracker could have been planted on the car in the hospital lot, though Liam doubted Tyler would have missed that.

Liam's phone rang with the tune he'd assigned Grey. His heart leapt. His hand shook as he pulled the phone from its pocket and hit Talk. He went for casual. "Hey."

"I'm sorry I left like that. I know you're only trying to help."

He wanted to ease her, to tell her it didn't matter. All he managed was a shuddering breath that sounded too fragile for comfort to his ears.

"I got your message. I paid cash for the room I'm in. I'm safe."

The blind in her room shifted and her outline came into view. Liam was far enough away she shouldn't see him. Just in case, he turned toward the water. As he did, he noticed the man in black pull out a phone.

Liam's neck tingled. He needed to warn her. "Grey, I have to tell you something you're not going to like."

"What?"

"I'm not sure you're as safe as you think."

"What do you mean?"

The man returned the phone to his pocket and then opened a small case sitting beside him. A moment later he raised a gun.

Everything in Liam shifted and trained instinct kicked in. "Get down," he snapped at Grey as he charged the man.

A muffled pop sounded. The bullet was released. Grey screamed and hit the blinds as she dove, or fell, to the floor.

With his left hand Liam stowed his phone in his pack and with his right he pulled his weapon. "FBI! Freeze!"

Predictably, the man leapt to his feet and began running, leaving his case behind.

The man turned with his weapon trained. Liam did a forward roll and on the way back up he took his aim. They both squeezed their triggers.

The shooter's bullet landed a few inches to Liam's left. Liam's landed in the man's leg. "Freeze," he ordered again as he slipped his gun back into its pouch.

The shooter stumbled but didn't stop. Rage surged. Liam took a flying leap and tackled the shooter as he again began to turn with his gun raised. The impact knocked the shooter's weapon from his hand. They went down in a flurry of sand.

"I said freeze," Liam snarled as he straddled the perp's back. Grabbing the man's hands, Liam held them in one hand

and encouraged the shooter to eat dirt while reaching for the zip-tie cuffs with his free one.

"You shot me."

"You're under arrest for illegally discharging a weapon in city limits, public endangerment, and as soon as I check your phone I'm sure I'll add attempted murder and conspiracy to commit murder." He jerked the man to his feet and pushed him back the way they'd come.

Ignoring the curious onlookers, Liam retrieved the shooter's gun and case when they passed them.

"I called Aidan," Grey said from a few feet away, phone in hand and arms hugging herself. Blood dripped from scratches on her face and neck. They appeared to be superficial and she wasn't acting as if they bothered her. He took it as a good sign, though he knew it could just mean she was in shock.

The shooter turned toward Grey and stared. "He said you'd be an easy target. Next time you won't be so lucky."

"Who hired you?"

The man said nothing else. Liam shoved him on and avoided Grey's gaze. Whatever he might find in her eyes, if he looked, he knew it would break him and he had to focus.

He wanted to throttle her for leaving and putting herself in danger, but he also wanted to pull her close and hug her. Jessup's man could have caught up with her at any point in the day. She was damn lucky Liam had followed her.

"He'll be here in a few minutes," she finished.

Liam nodded and shoved his limping captive ahead of him toward the car. Grey fell into step with Liam, but thankfully stayed silent. He had a lot to say, but not with their present audience. Instead, he recited the Miranda as they went.

Aidan pulled into the lot at the same time they rounded the corner. When his brother exited his car and rounded the hood, Liam shoved the shooter toward his brother. "Trunk."

Aidan hit the button on the key fob with one hand while catching the perp's arm with the other. "You seem to have irritated Agent Burgess."

"He shot me."

"Self-defense," Liam said from behind the trunk where he put the shooter's gun and case in evidence bags.

He returned with a roll of bandages. He'd prefer to let the asshole bleed out, but they had a tendency to get more out of people when they weren't bleeding or passing out from low blood pressure. Besides, though they all bought black leather seats for easier cleanup, Aidan preferred to minimize the amount of blood in his car.

While he wrapped the man's leg, Liam recapped everything for Aidan. Grey stood a little back, but close. Nothing squashed a desire for freedom like flying bullets.

Chapter Ten

It took another hour to wrap up the scene. Aidan took the now silent shooter to the hospital for treatment and then would take him in for booking and interrogation. Ava came to take Grey's statement while it was fresh and got her checked out by the paramedics who had come on scene. Breck was on the phone with the director and the U.S. Marshals Service, filling everyone in. Kieralyn worked with a team to process the motel room while Liam worked with a team on the beach. They mapped the scene and recovered the bullets.

The whole time, Liam wanted nothing more than to be alone with Grey. Touching her, holding her, kissing her. After seeing the shattered glass of her door, the bullet imbedded in the wall beyond and the glass scratches on her face he needed some reassurance. He could only imagine that she needed some.

"We're finished, Agent Burgess," a tech said. "We'll get everything back to the office and have it catalogued by morning."

"Thank you." He thanked Kieralyn and made his way to Ava's car where Grey sat behind a dark-tinted window. Every step landed harder, jarred him with the need he'd been shoving down since seeing the shooter raise his gun. His control wasn't going to last much longer. "How is she?"

"Shaken."

"Her cuts?"

"Superficial. She's got fast reflexes."

His jaw flexed. "She wouldn't have needed them if she'd trusted me."

"She did trust you," Ava assured. "She said she didn't know where you were, but you said get down and she did. She heard the bullet breeze past."

Ava curled her fingers around his hand and locked her gaze with his. He calmed quickly and the relief was so great he didn't care if H came after him for letting her use her empathic ability on him. Much.

"She's had a rough time," Ava said no doubt knowing he was thinking clearer. "I know a little something about that."

Liam winced. Ava was so strong and settled with H and she fit so smoothly with the team he often forgot about her background. If Grey had gone through anything close...

Ava squeezed his hand gently, again pulling away his rising stress. "Keep being patient."

"That's becoming tougher every day."

"Start by asking where she'd prefer to stay and know that H's lab is an option." She winked encouragingly. "It's very secure."

That was an understatement. H saw government conspiracy in almost everything. When he'd escaped captivity a few years earlier, he made damn sure he was protected from anything that might come his way. He just hadn't seen Ava coming. "Thank you."

She winked again and opened the door that concealed Grey.

Liam had seen a lot of looks on Grey's face in the short time he'd known her. Joy. Mischief. Sadness. Worry. Guilt. Loneliness. Surrender. Passion.

The patch of skin between her eyebrows pinched. Her fingers drew lines on her legs. The clearest clue to her thoughts though was in her eyes. Even when her words said one thing, her eyes always conveyed truth. Now was no different and her eyes were filled with contrition. Apologetic agony.

Sitting in Ava's front seat, pale against the dark leather, Grey broke his heart. Then she sniffed as if she'd been crying. That shattered him.

"Will you come with me, Grey? Please." He wasn't sure if he'd ever said please to her any other time. He only knew how much he needed her with him and if a please could make that happen...

She stayed still and silent. He offered a hand, but his insides trembled with the need to drop to his knees and beg. She licked her lips and then placed her hand in his. The shaking touch reached into his chest and squeezed. Tears of triumph burned the backs of his eyes, but he swallowed them. Instead, he silently curled his fingers around hers and helped her from the car.

They didn't speak as he led her to his car, opened her door and then closed it behind her. Rounding the hood, looking at her the whole way, he reminded himself of his mother's advice about letting her go and Ava's about going slow. They both contradicted everything he wanted and the outcome of his internal war was still undecided.

He started the car.

Every emotion he'd shoved aside and down since seeing that gun, everything Ava had tried to pull out of him, bubbled to the surface. They rolled over each other beneath his skin until he felt like angry serpents were fighting for dominance.

He turned off the car.

He was accustomed to knowing what he wanted and what needed to be done, but Grey knocked him off stride.

"Liam?"

He shook his head. Unable to trust whatever he might say, he dropped his forehead to the steering wheel and tried to breathe steadily, but it was no use. Every inhale and exhale was a jagged movement of air that delivered little healing power to his cells. He needed to stash Grey in a safe corner where nothing bad could touch her and then he needed to pound the shit out of something.

He saw no other answer, but that one wouldn't happen.

She rested her hand, only the fingertips really, on his shoulder. "Will you take me home?"

He fought against the pressure of tears that surged with face-heating pleasure. When he was sure he could keep his eyes dry, he raised his head and looked at Grey. She shouldn't feel ashamed of wanting the freedom to make her own choices, yet her eyes were still darkened by heartbreaking contrition.

"Is that where you really want to go, or are you saying this because you think you owe me?"

"I left to keep people out of danger and look what happened. I made everything worse."

"So, because you think you owe me."

She shrugged, but didn't answer.

"Where would you go if you didn't have to worry about any repercussions, Grey? Where did you go to feel safe when you were Opal?"

"The beach." She laughed, but it was a sad one. "There was a private section of beach I used to visit. Rocks blocked it off from the rest of the world. As screwed up as things got, it was always perfect."

He nodded and turned the car back on. He couldn't take her to the escape that had been Opal's, but he could give her the next best thing because he suddenly knew of the perfect place to keep her safe. At least for the night.

Grey tried to imagine what might be in Liam's head. The scenarios ranged from hate to rage and allowed for other possibilities. She had asked him to take her home because she owed him. She had owed him gratitude for looking out for her. Now she owed him for saving her life even if she didn't know how he'd known where to find her.

He said nothing as he turned away from home. At least nothing to her. He pulled his phone from the pack he'd set between the seats and dialed a number. The call was answered quickly and Ava's voice filled the car.

"Liam."

"Ava. You remember that option?"

"Of course. Let me get H."

A moment later a strong, male voice came through the speakers. Liam muttered acknowledgements as H gave him instructions on bypassing a security system. Even after he ended the call he said nothing to Grey. He didn't even look at her as he drove to a secret place.

Thankfully, the confinement of miserable silence in the car seemed to be a short one. He pulled into an empty parking lot of an unimpressive white building. There was no sign to announce what the place was or suggest why they were there instead of at Liam's.

Like he'd taken to doing every time, he leaned over her and opened her door. The brush of his arm on her breast, the closeness of his face, in those beating moments, quickened passion's pulse.

That made her think about the promise he'd made that morning about kissing. He would kiss her once a day, but he hadn't kissed her yet and the day was almost over.

Liam pulled back and took his pack as he exited the car. The chill of rejection froze her. He wouldn't be kissing her; she'd killed the desire.

Grey moved mechanically as she got out of the car and followed him to the building's main entrance. He entered a code into the door pad and when she was inside with him he entered it again.

The moonlight shone through the large windows, allowing her to see the basic leather chairs and couches and the reception desk. Turning from the stark entrance, she followed Liam down the dark hall in a creepy silence and couldn't help but ask, "What is this place?"

"Safe," was his only answer as he went in and flipped on a light in a locker room.

The place was white, cold. She wouldn't have described it as safe, though Liam didn't seem concerned with what she may be thinking as he grabbed some towels and blankets from a cabinet. Maintaining his silence, he led her back out, flipping the light off as they left.

Down the hall, he pushed a quick release bar on the back door and stepped outside. Here, for the first time, Grey noticed the sound of the ocean. She only saw trees, though, until Liam turned down a sand path.

The water grew louder. A short time later they stepped onto a beach. It was a private one lit only by the moon and stars. It was a slightly larger version of the one she used to visit.

"Liam. Seriously?"

He shrugged with the blankets and towels still in hand. "Ava's soon-to-be husband keeps this a well-guarded secret. I thought we'd sleep here tonight and figure out the rest in the morning."

It was the most he'd said to her all night and, damn it, the words made her want to cry. He was backing down from his need to call the shots and offering her a night in a haven. With her throat thick, she went to Liam and pushed up on her toes to kiss his cheek. "It's perfect." *You're perfect.*

"I'm glad." He swallowed and stepped back. "Go explore or sit and stare or whatever. No one will see you except me."

Grey wanted to say something, to explain how much his thoughtfulness meant to her. To ask what he was thinking and how he'd known where to find her and that she was in danger. The words wouldn't come. With a brush of her fingers along his arm she walked toward the water, stepping out of her shoes as she went.

She glanced back. Liam spread the blankets out and then set the towels on a corner. A part of her wanted him to join her at the water, but she didn't ask. Instead of joining her, he sat on the blankets and watched.

She had messed up by leaving, possibly enough to drive a wedge between them, but the man had just given her the one thing she'd missed most since leaving five years earlier. She was going to enjoy it and do as he suggested. She'd worry about the rest tomorrow.

Turning to the water, Grey unfastened her capris and let them slip down her legs. She tugged her shirt over her head and dropped it. If she didn't have an audience she might have stripped all the way, but Liam was watching.

She smiled. What did it matter that Liam watched? He'd seen her naked before, and she hadn't been shy.

He was watching, and she wanted him to kiss her. She was going to remind him he wanted to kiss her.

Grey reached around, popped the bra hooks and eased the straps down her arms. She dropped the satin torture device and sighed. Arousal trembled to life as she tucked her fingertips beneath the waist of her panties and pushed them down.

Exhilaration flooded her. With an audience of one, an audience who made her body sing with a touch, she sauntered closer to the water. The wet sand was cool and smooth between her toes. The gentle waves as they rushed in and out swept her skin like a lover's caress.

The farther she went the more constant and persistent that touch became. Cool water brushed between her legs. Heated ripples of desire tightened her stomach. She was ready, eager, for an orgasm that would come so easily. Indulgence would wait.

She went farther, embracing every inch of water that pulled her deeper and deeper into its embrace. She stopped when the slippery surface rested along the bottoms of her breasts.

Stretching her arms out, she rested her hands palm up on the water. Moonlight bathed her in perfection until all that existed was bliss.

Violence and death, lies and betrayals, nightmares and impossible dreams all slipped away. They flowed out the tips of her fingertips and were washed away. Freedom had never been so real. And it wasn't something she'd had to fight for. It was a gift she'd been handed by a man who understood more than she could have hoped.

Greycen Craig was a skin Opal Donovan had donned out of necessity. The conflicting women in her head had pulled at her ever since, but now, the salt in the ocean waters exfoliated the old. It buffed away the shell she'd never felt comfortable in and gave her space to discover herself.

She wasn't only Opal any more than she was only Grey. She was a work in progress and her newest revelation lay in knowing exactly what she wanted. At the moment she wanted Liam to kiss her.

She smiled as she approached the beach. She closed the distance between them, springing off the balls of her feet. She was naked and he was looking. The awareness of those facts preceded every step until she stepped onto the blanket, dripping wet. With a swallow, Grey stepped over his legs and lowered herself until she straddled his lap.

He tilted his head just the tiniest bit. "Enjoy yourself?"

She kissed his right temple. "More..." then his left, "...than you..." then his right cheekbone, "...may..." his left, "...ever..." his right jaw, "...know." His left. Grey eased back and looked at him seriously. "I need to apologize for running away when you've only tried to help. I want to be able to explain myself and tell you everything that's happened."

"But you can't."

She shook her head. "I can tell you I feel lighter, more at peace."

"H and Ava swear the water here is healing."

"I feel lighter, but I also know the stress and fear will come back."

"And when it does you'll start arguing again."

"Or try to run," she admitted.

He moved his hands to her hips. "You won't get far."

"You'll tell me later how you came to be on that beach."

He shrugged. "Maybe."

He *would* tell her; she'd make sure of it. Later. "Right now I want something else."

"What, Grey? What do you want?"

"I want that kiss you promised this morning."

Chapter Eleven

Grey was wet, naked and beneath his hands. He wasn't breaking the touch after craving it for so long. Fun didn't need to be out of the picture, though. Liam checked his watch by twisting his wrist and leaning left a little. "I still have thirty minutes before the day is over."

She wiggled a little, which brushed her breasts against his chest. She wasn't big, barely a handful, but size didn't matter with perfection like hers.

"It's been a rough day, Liam. I think you'd agree."

Beyond rough and things weren't easing up in some regards. "A rough day is no reason to rush things."

"Then kiss me and make it last."

"Is that all you're asking for, Grey? Do you want it to stop at a kiss?" He had to have hit his head when he tackled her shooter. Why else would he hold out?

"I'm asking you to kiss me. I'm not sure I'm ready for everything else you do to me."

As admissions went hers blew him away in its honesty. He had a weakness for honesty. Hell, he had a weakness for Grey.

"Are you sure you're ready for my definition of a kiss?"

"Yes." She moved closer, definitely close enough to feel how she affected him, not that she should be surprised there.

"Okay." He grinned as he leaned in. If he had to stop at a kiss he was going to make it good for them both.

Copying her kisses when she'd first straddled his lap, a move that had hardened him more than watching her undress or enjoy herself in the water, he kissed her right temple. Liam granted her nothing more than a close-mouthed peck on the temple, but she leaned into it.

He eased away and kissed her other temple. Again he lingered just long enough for her to lean into it. Pulling away, he moved from her right cheekbone to her left, taking his time to savor the lingering scent of her morning shower.

Grey sighed as he placed his lips to her right jaw. Unlike the last caresses he opened his mouth this time. He blew a warm breath along the edge of her jaw and ear. She squirmed. He grinned as a shiver slid over his arms. Then he kissed her left jawbone and again blew a long breath before closing his lips.

She arched her back, shifting the silk of her skin beneath his fingers. They curled of their own accord into the flesh of her waist. It wasn't enough. None of it was enough.

Her nipples pressed against his chest, begged for attention. A flick of his fingers would be cheating, worse, a flick would lead to a squeeze, which would lead to all out groping.

Poking the tip of his tongue between his lips he ran it from her jaw down to the hollow of her neck. "You taste like salty sea," he murmured.

She dropped her head back on a sigh. Her pussy rubbed the length of his dick. His eyes rolled back in his head. Liam bit down on his tongue to keep from sinking his teeth into her.

"Liam."

"I'm just getting warmed up."

Her moaned response was all the encouragement he needed to continue. Her sides quivered beneath his gliding hands. When she rested her hands on his shoulders he allowed himself the briefest brush of thumb against nipple. She jumped. Power surged in his veins and melted his muscles.

He gripped her shoulders and eased her back. Cravings crashed in her gaze, mirror reflections of his own. He ached with his body's tightening need to plunge deep. Her pelvis rotated forward, teasing him. He'd deserve a box of medals if he held out all night.

Liam growled as he swept in and claimed her mouth. Even if she asked for sex he didn't have a condom so they'd have to stop, but he'd be damned if he didn't yearn for it. She opened for him, angled left while he angled right. Tongues danced. Lips brushed.

Grey rolled her hips again. Her heated wetness seeped through his shorts. His hips rose to meet hers. She grabbed his head and pulled him closer, deepening the kiss. He explored the inner recesses of her mouth, slid his tongue between her gums and teeth.

She ground against him, moving faster. The lining of his running shorts became slippery with her arousal as she neared orgasm.

Liam ripped his mouth from hers and sank his teeth into her neck. She rubbed herself against him. He suckled on her neck.

Orgasm built, drew closer and closer with each panting breath. The moment he began to go over the ledge, Grey arched her back and pressed herself close.

The layers of his shorts muffled the flexing pulses of her orgasm, but he was too attuned to her to miss them. He moved his mouth back to hers and kissed her gently until her pulses eased. He'd promised to stop at kissing and while he wasn't sure if he'd kept that promise he couldn't regret it, because no kiss had ever been so hot.

Grey rested her head on Liam's shoulder and huddled close as he pulled the spare blanket over her. The darkness, gratefully, hid the flush heating her cheeks. She'd asked him to stop at kissing and then she'd rubbed herself off on him.

No mixed messages there. "Liam?"

"Mmm?"

"How did you know where I was?"

"I planted a tracker in your car."

"Oh?"

"And in your phone."

"I see."

"And I bugged you."

"What? How?" She lurched up, but he pulled her back. When she'd again settled against him he traced a finger along the back of her neck.

"Kieralyn's husband created a listening device that can be stuck to your skin and looks like a hair."

"How long have you been listening to me?"

"Only after you checked in at the motel."

"I see. And when did you bug me?"

"While you were sleeping that first night after you'd almost left." His fingers moved along her neck and over her shoulder. The post-orgasm excitement that had settled began to rise again, rush through her blood.

"Why? I had agreed to stay." Not that she had, but she hadn't snuck out.

"I was scared." Liam rubbed his face against the top of her head. His heart pounded hard and erratic beneath her ear. "I was scared you'd change your mind. I wanted to know I could find you."

"That's why you let me go, because you'd know where I was."

"No. I let you go because you wanted freedom and trusted me to give it to you. The bugs just made watching you walk a little less painful."

She chuckled. "Like I could hurt you."

In a blur, Liam rolled Grey to her back and towered over her. His gaze bored into her. Unblinking. Hard.

She swallowed.

"You scare me, Grey, because I'm afraid I'll mess up when it matters most because of worrying about you. You have an eerie power over me and yes, when you ran from me at the house, each step away was a bullet to my heart."

"I had no idea."

"I didn't want you to. I still don't."

"Then why did you?" She tugged at his shirt. He'd been so hard and rigid after the incident. The kiss being the one exception.

"I don't want to lie to you, but I really don't want to be left behind wondering if you're safe. Especially since we know Jessup has people coming for you."

Grey nodded. She still wasn't ready to think about being Liam's wife or how unsuited she was for his world, but she couldn't deny him.

"I won't run again. I have no doubt I'll freak out on you again, and I still think I'm bringing unnecessary danger to your door, but I promise not to leave again until we're certain it's safe."

"You could be stuck with me for a while."

"I know."

"You may meet more of my family."

"I'll be nice." She knew that wasn't what he meant, but the other was something else she couldn't think about.

"I'm not lying about who you are."

"That doesn't mean you have to tack 'my wife' to every introduction."

"No, but I happen to like the sound of it."

"Liam." The man was a wall of stubborn. And then he did something disarming like smile with a gleam in his gaze that rattled her resolve.

He smiled with that gleam and inclined his head like he was acknowledging a point. "But—" he lifted her left hand and pressed a kiss to the diamond ring he'd given her in Vegas, "—if you promise to stay and let us help you until you and I both agree you're safe I will promise not to introduce you as my wife."

His lips over her finger, over the ring she'd been unwilling to remove, were reminders of the night she'd agreed to marry him. He'd kissed her the same way after slipping the ring on the first time. "I feel like you've left room for a loophole in there."

He smiled. "Do we have a deal?"

"On one condition."

"Name it."

"Take me home. I may be easygoing but I'm not a girl who sleeps nude under the stars."

"On one hand that's sad to hear."

"But on the other?" She might have just rediscovered the fun Liam she'd met in Vegas.

"I wouldn't mind seeing you nude on my bed." With a grin he grabbed his backpack, wrapped her in a blanket and carried her toward the car.

"My clothes!"

"We'll get them later."

"They're the only ones I have left." Everything she had had been left in her car and motel room.

"Fine." He set her on her feet and hurried to gather her things. Even if she did have something else to wear she would've wanted her things picked up. Otherwise she'd be embarrassed by the idea of Ava's fiancé gathering her underwear.

Liam returned with her clothes and the towels and blankets he'd borrowed. "Better?"

"Yes," she replied sweetly. "Thank you."

"Sure thing." He walked toward the building's back entrance. "Though I'd rather be carrying you."

"You're a complex man, Liam Burgess."

He coded into the back door and headed to the locker room. "I prefer my naked wife in my arms instead of her clothes. Nothing complex there."

"Liam, you promised."

"I promised not to introduce you to everyone as my wife. I never promised to pretend you weren't."

"I knew there were loopholes."

"Stick around long enough and maybe you'll learn to work them in your favor. Now..." He tossed her shirt and capris over his shoulder, tucked her bra and panties in his pocket and opened his empty arms. "Shall we go?"

"I am perfectly capable of walking." She angled her shoulders away from him as she passed.

He swept her off her feet, curled her close and headed to the front of the building. The feel of his arms and body supporting her were almost hypnotic enough to banish her free will.

"I really can walk."

"Don't take this the wrong way." He paused long enough to code out of the front door. "But putting aside how sexy your walk is, I've seen enough of it for the next little while."

He wasn't letting her off the hook easily, which she probably deserved. It made her wonder if she had hurt him. Did he really care that much? If he did, why? How long could it really last?

"I made a promise."

"More than one."

"Are you going to forgive me for leaving?"

"There's nothing to forgive, though it's going to take some time to forget."

"I don't think we ever forget. At least not the big stuff."

He set her on her feet beside the car. Framing her face with his hands he leaned in close. Her breath caught at the raw sincerity in his gaze.

"Greycen Craig Burgess, you should consider yourself big stuff. *Nothing* you say or do will be easily forgotten."

She swallowed and hoped nothing else would be said. Anything more would minimize his admission. Ready or not, she was falling and no amount of fairy dust would save her.

Chapter Twelve

Grey hid at the top of the stairs and listened as Liam answered the door. A woman's cheery laugh reached her clearly.

"It never matters what you've changed, Liam, a part of me always feels dirty when I come in here." The woman talked fast and sounded as chipper as her laugh. "At least until I see the sun. I love the light all the new windows let in."

"The place changes with the people in it. And you were never dirty."

"Maybe. Speaking of people, when is Lana coming over?"

"Anytime."

"Would it be okay if I invited Lori over?" The woman laughed again. "She's curious to see what changes you've made."

"If Grey's fine with it you know I am."

"Thanks, Liam. So when do I get to meet the mysterious Grey? Where is she?"

"She'll be down soon. It was a long night. Is that...?"

"Yes."

"Why don't you go to the kitchen and make sure the coffee's ready." His tone shifted to humor. "She's more talkative after a few cups."

"You cooking too? I haven't eaten yet."

"We'll see."

His voice sounded closer. A few quick moments later he stepped onto the top landing and looked at her with that humored smile of his that made him so sexy. "Grey."

"Who's here?"

"A friend." He lifted a suitcase. "She brought you some clothes."

It wasn't any suitcase. It was a Louis Vuitton. Grey backed away. Hand-me-downs were bad, but when they came from a case like that... They wouldn't be her kind of clothes.

He cocked his head and lifted the case a little. "You can't want to wear those clothes again today."

"It's better than whatever is in there."

He set the case at her feet. "When you're finished making snap judgments like a clichéd snob you might find something in here that's to your liking."

Saying nothing else, he turned and walked downstairs. His departing chastisement shamed her into carrying the bag into the bedroom to see what had been brought over.

The suitcase held a few options. Conservative class, like what she'd worn to the hospital, and edgy with a gothic flair, like what she'd have worn as Opal. Beneath those was a third option. Dramatic comfort.

She'd missed Opal's clothes so much that while it was smarter to choose the style of Grey, she struggled with the desire to revisit her old self.

Ten minutes later, dressed in the third option of jeans made of the softest denim she'd ever felt and a tie-dye T-shirt with rips strategically placed over a shoulder and the left ribcage, and a blingy skull, she headed back toward the stairs. An apology, something she seemed to be giving more than she liked, formed in her mind. Whoever was downstairs, she'd gone to some trouble for Grey's benefit.

The doorbell rang, loud and majestic, as she descended the last step. She looked from the door to the hall that led to the kitchen, uncomfortable answering the door.

"That will be Lana." The woman's voice reached her. "I'll get it."

Footsteps, lightly muffled, preceded the woman. She moved fast. Grey looked for a place to hide, but didn't find one in time. A blonde, exquisite from head to toe in casual glamour, came into view.

Grey gasped.

The blonde looked up and smiled. "Hi."

Grey could only nod.

Recognition would have been instant even without the vibrant red streak in the front of her wavy hair. Kami Evans. After a guest spot on an award-winning television show, the public had responded so favorably Kami Evans had become a regular. The show had never been better than it was with her. Grey waited all week for Friday night to watch the show, and now, Kami Evans was in front of her. And she'd brought a bag of clothes for Grey.

A sweet smile lifted her lips as she turned and opened the door. "Lana. Come in."

The woman Kami called Lana set two bags inside the door. They embraced and then Kami pulled back, pointed to the bags. "Thank you for bringing those."

"Anything for Aidan and Liam."

Grey tried to connect the pieces of information she'd been given since returning. She didn't know how Kami Evans fit into Liam's world; she wouldn't have missed that. Lana was marrying Aidan and was the FBI director's daughter, but she seemed familiar beyond that.

"No big stories to chase down?"

Lana glanced up to Grey and smiled as she answered Kami. "None that can't wait a day. Or more."

Lana Quinn. Top award-winning reporter in Miami. Grey always read Lana's articles first. Sometimes she even kept them. Before her, in what could only be described as a mansion, a home Liam wanted her to think of as her own, stood two of Miami's most important women.

Lana grabbed the two bags she'd brought in and looked at Grey again. "You must be Grey. I'm Aidan's fiancée, Lana Quinn."

"Hi." Grey's voice cracked, forcing her to clear her throat.

"And I'm Kami Evans."

Grey lifted a hand in a slight wave. "I know who you are." God. It was like being slammed back to high school where she wasn't sure why the popular kids were talking to her.

Kami smiled and took one of the bags from Lana. "Then join us. We'll kick Liam out of the house and do what women do best."

"Talk about men." Lana laughed and shook her bag. "And play with chocolate."

Grey found herself sinking deeper and deeper into a world she needed to escape. Then it hit her. She was Alice and this was Liam's wonderland.

At least it came with chocolate.

A little later, a Disney movie played on the big screen in the living room and the kitchen smelled of chocolate confections, some prettier than others depending on who'd done them.

Lori Mullins, owner of a local wedding planning business, had joined them. Lana and Kami had given a tour of the home, especially showing off the changes Liam had made to the lab that was now called a safe room. Liam had said Grey was safe. She actually felt it.

With the tour over and the gossip in swing, Lori sat on an island barstool with a sketchpad, working on a wedding dress. Swearing she couldn't boil water without burning it, she designated herself as the taste tester.

Lana was pretty adept, but Kami, well, Kami wasn't very good in the kitchen.

"Grey, we may need to add you to our database of caterers," Lori said after tasting a white chocolate truffle with a blueberry drizzle. "These would work perfectly for so many of the weddings we plan."

"It's just a hobby." Grey shrugged away the idea of owning a business, of being a chef. Thinking about past dreams could pass the time, but nothing so settled as a real career existed in her future.

"It's a gift, and it's something to think about when your sister's recovered."

Grey had wondered if everyone who walked into her life knew about her not being whom she said she was, but Liam had assured her Lana was the only one in the house who knew about the WitSec ID. He couldn't guarantee that Kami didn't know about them being married, but he'd shrugged it off saying the only thing that mattered was her safety. Then he'd assured her she would be safe while he was gone. Especially with Lori in the house. She'd tried to ask about that, but he'd refused to answer.

"It's a gift I don't seem to have." Kami laughed as the chocolate she was trying to drizzle over some dipped strawberries came out in clumps.

She'd managed to get chocolate in her hair and on her neck and there was a huge smear across the bust of her apron. Seeing her look less than high-def perfect was fun.

"If I did social media, I would so ask for a picture of you right now." Grey smiled as she moved to help Kami. She could almost stop thinking of her as Kami Evans, actress, but not quite.

Lana grabbed her arm to stop her with one hand while grabbing her phone with the other. "Well I do social media and I won't ask for the picture."

Before she finished her declaration Lana had snapped a picture and was uploading it to Twitter. Teehee-ing, she turned the phone to show Grey.

@ActressKamiEvans is experimenting with chocolate. Where r the men when u need them? #girltime

Grey laughed. She'd done a lot of that since the women had kicked Liam out and started unloading bags. At moments it felt like they'd been friends for years, like there were no differences in their social classes or backgrounds. Those brief moments would become treasured memories when she walked away.

"I'm glad Breck isn't on Twitter," Kami said. "He'd see that and start making demands." She chuckled as she set her bag down and typed a response to Lana's tweet.

Lana smirked. "You'll indulge them either way. Who knows, maybe with a little more help from Grey you'll be less messy."

"Life's messy. That's where the fun is." Lori winked.

Kami wiped at the chocolate on her neck, smearing it more. "Says the woman who never looks less than flawless."

"Image is everything," Lori said with her head high. "It pains me to say it, but that was one thing Madame X had right. Even when you're pretending, if you project the right image, people will believe you're who you say you are."

Guilt stabbed Grey. Her entire existence was a pretense. An image. A façade. And she was pulling more people into it. Worse, they were people she liked and didn't want to hurt.

"I disagree," Lana said as her phone rang. She continued talking as she answered. "Eventually we all have to take off our masks and let people see the real us. Only then do we learn who we really are. Isn't that right, babe?" she asked the caller who had to be Aidan.

Grey left Lana to her call and tried not to think about being unmasked. These high-class women would never accept her if they knew the things she'd done. Instead, she stepped behind Kami and wrapped a hand over hers to help with the chocolate bag.

"Who's Madame X?" she asked between giving pointers to Kami.

"A bitch," Kami and Lori muttered in unison with a matching tone of hatred.

Lana ended the call, having listened more than talked to Aidan, and saved Grey with an explanation. "Madame X ran an escort agency. This house was her base of operations until Breck and the team took her down."

"This house." Grey waved a hand. "Liam said he got a killer's deal." She shivered. "Did she kill people here?"

"No, but she did orchestrate a few hits from here."

"How can you talk about it so casually like it's not creepy to be in a killer's kitchen?"

"We've learned to let it go. Counseling can also help." Lori set her pencil down and looked directly at Grey. "I was a spy sent here to work a case. I didn't realize the agency I was with was corrupt until I fell in love with one of Madame X's clients. The real trigger was when an innocent man died because of me."

Lori had been a spy? Like Sydney Bristow in *Alias*? That explained why Liam had said she could protect Grey. Focusing on the story instead of Lori's history, Grey asked, "Who was he?"

"My stepbrother," Kami said quietly as if she still mourned him. "They made it look like a suicide, which I didn't believe. So I went undercover as a call girl to prove he was murdered."

"That's how she met Breck," Lana said. "And through Kami being here we met Ava. And through Breck investigating his best friend's connection to the case we met Lori."

"How are Lori and Breck's best friend connected?"

"He's the client I fell in love with and the second man who was supposed to die because of me," Lori stated matter-of-factly. "Almost did. He's also my fiancé."

"How are you two friends?" Grey asked Lori and Kami. "And with all that happened how can you stand to be here? In this place?"

"Because as screwed up as our journey together began, and trust me when I say we've been through some heavy shit, Kami and I found love as a result."

"And met Ava, who is seriously awesome." Kami spoke slowly, concentrating on the drizzle. She was almost getting it. "And through her we met H and Simon."

"And they took down a corrupt agency and granted a man and his sister the greatest gift they could have hoped for."

Lana's wrap-up sounded like a much bigger story, so Grey didn't ask about the gift. Though she was curious.

"So how can you be in this house?"

"The house wasn't evil. Its owner was. We wouldn't have the lives we do if not for what started here with Lori." Kami grinned as she finished a successful drizzle. "She was bringing us all together even before we knew she existed."

And Liam made sure they had the chance to form happier memories in the house. He'd taken their unconventional beginning and turned it into something positive and reaffirming. He was trying to do the same with Grey, with their marriage. She just wasn't so sure he'd be as successful with her.

"Hey!" Lana smacked her hand on the counter, making them all jump, and then pointed at Lori. "You said fiancé. Did you finally accept Trevor's proposals?"

"Proposals?" Grey asked.

"It's a game they play," Kami said out of the corner of her mouth while watching Lori. "He asks her daily and she never answers."

"I'm just trying it on." Lori shrugged. "I love him but I can't stop wondering if he's too good for me."

Grey's eyes widened. The woman had pulled up in a luxurious convertible and was the picture of elegance. She fit in with Kami and Lana as if they'd been friends forever, yet she had the same doubts about belonging. "How can that be?"

"I have no family," Lori said. "I've done horrible things, including murder and prostitution."

"Both under the guise of helping our country," Kami stated.

"I nearly got Trevor killed. Then I vanished. Now I reject him over and over. Why would he want to be with me? Why should I shackle him to me?"

It was the same kind of dilemma Grey faced with Liam. Shitty background. Unusual beginning. Long absence. Rejection after reunion. Images weren't everything, because if they were she wouldn't have found anything in common with the women sharing the kitchen with her.

"None of that was under your control and Trevor knows it. Even if it was, it's in the past. Do you really want to miss out on whatever greatness is in store for you by continuing to reject him?"

Kami's challenge was aimed at Lori, but it hit a sour note in Grey. Did she want to miss out? What exactly might she be missing out on?

Speculation sucked, but she was pulled from further conversation by her ringing phone. The number on the display shot through her, awakening dread.

"Grey?"

"It's the hospital," she answered Lana automatically. Her thumb trembled as it neared the Talk button. She was shaking fully as she lifted the cell. "This is Grey."

Everything changed with three words and a flurry of movement.

"Ruby's waking up," the caller said. They said more, but she only heard the three words she'd waited to hear. *Ruby's waking up.*

Grey's knees went weak. Lana hurried forward and grabbed her. Kami pulled a barstool close. Lori got a washcloth and ran it under the water.

Whatever else was said about Ruby went unheard beneath the buzz of emotions until Lana took the phone from her. Lori rubbed the rag over Grey's face and neck, but it only made her skin wet.

Someone, maybe Lana, told someone, maybe Kami, to call Liam.

That rabbit hole was looking more like a tornado and what she needed most was a wizard with a miracle.

Chapter Thirteen

Liam had been on Grey duty for four days, counting his time watching Ruby, but as much as he adored her, as badly as he wanted her to fall in love with him and understand that his life wasn't as fancy as she thought, he ached with the need for answers. When he arrived at the office, he only knew what his calls from the car had netted him. Simon was on Ruby watch and Tyler was running the data they had.

It wasn't enough and Liam was ready for battle.

The office that was reserved exclusively for the Specialized Crimes Unit was abuzz with activity. Ava and Kieralyn weren't in, but men sat at their desks on the phones. Breck was in his office with another man in a suit who gestured wildly.

Aidan stood from his desk and approached Liam. "How's Grey?"

"Safe at home with Kami, Lana and Lori."

"Good."

"What's going on here? You get anything out of Grey's shooter?"

Aidan shook his head. "Nothing yet. He's under guard at the hospital. Kieralyn and Ava are heading over to talk to him now."

"What about the lab? Anything on prints or ballistics?" Liam asked.

"Nothing useful yet. The gun was unregistered and the shooter has no prints." Aidan pointed at the men using the girls' desks. "They're working to verify him as McKay, though it's doubtful that's his name."

"Who are they?"

"U.S. Marshals. The one currently arguing with Breck for jurisdiction is Micah. He wants Grey back with him."

"Then they know something they're not sharing."

"Don't they always?"

The double glass doors to their space opened behind Liam. He turned and watched Director Quinn enter. Graying at the temples, power preceded his every step, and it was only partly due to his size and the way he dressed. More than anything, Director Quinn carried himself as a man not to be crossed, and as a result few people did.

"Liam, where's Ms. Craig?"

"My house. Safe."

He turned his gaze on Aidan. "And Lana?"

"At Liam's with Kami, Grey and Lori Mullins."

Director Quinn nodded once and then lowered his voice. "Get an agent over there."

"Are they in danger?" Liam's blood sped up. He reached for his phone.

"Possibly."

"I have one of Ian's bugs on Grey." When his brother and the director looked at him with suspicious gazes, Liam just shrugged. "Like you two wouldn't tag Lana twenty-four seven if you could get away with it."

"Do any of the women know about Ms. Craig's situation?"

"Lana."

The director nodded. "Aidan, call her. Tell her an agent is heading over and if she has an argument she can take it up with me. Liam, I want that device active and monitored."

"Yes, sir." Liam had already pushed the app icon to activate it. "What's going on?"

"Karl Jessup has escaped."

"I'll be the agent Lana should expect." Liam headed for the door not caring how close he was to the case. He only cared about getting back to Grey before anything bad could happen. Or before she heard about Jessup from someone else.

He had just settled behind the wheel of the car and gotten the tablet docked with Grey's bug activated when Aidan called. It was all Liam could do not to call Grey himself, but he didn't want to alarm her until he was close enough to stop her if she tried to run. He turned down the volume on the tablet, satisfied that they were gossiping happily, and answered. "Yeah?"

"Lana says they're fine and she'll keep an eye out until you get there."

Aidan lowered his voice as if he didn't want someone nearby to overhear. "You're not going to like what Marshal Carpenter's pushing for."

"She's not been checking in with him. He wants her back."

"How do you know that?"

"I tapped her phone. And I've been with her almost constantly."

Liam turned onto the entrance ramp and came almost immediately to a stop behind the car in front of him. The occasional traffic on the way home had never bothered him. Now, when he needed to get to Grey, when he needed to verify for himself she was safe, was not the time for delays.

"He's pushing, hard, to get her back into protection."

Liam's heart sank. "She won't do it." He hoped. "Not without helping Ruby first."

"He's prepared to move Ruby."

"She has to be willing. She can't sign that paperwork and Grey doesn't have a power of attorney over her."

"Breck made those points." Aidan paused a moment before continuing. "Carpenter says Ruby can walk when she's recovered if she doesn't want to stay hidden."

Traffic moved, but only at ten miles per hour. The news from Aidan, the softness of female conversation floating through the car, the impotence of sitting in traffic when he needed to act grated and built until Liam was wringing his hands on the wheel.

"He can't hide someone on a donor list."

"A point the director made, but if Grey's approved as a donor..."

"Ruby could be kept off the list." *Shit.* It was a valid angle Grey might want to consider. "How are they going to handle the doctors? Jessup's people could still track a coma patient disappearing from one hospital and another showing up somewhere else."

"They're the U.S. Marshals. They're used to spinning stories and making people vanish."

Not Grey. Not again. He wasn't losing her.

Driven by fear and frustration, Liam flipped on the emergency lights he'd had wired along the edge of the roof and pulled the car onto the shoulder. Grey would not make a decision about WitSec without him. She sure as hell wouldn't face Jessup alone.

His phone beeped with Caller ID. A quick glance showed Kami's smiling face. "Kami's calling," he said to Aidan. "Keep me in the loop."

He pressed Talk to switch from Aidan to Kami. The same urgency pressed in on him, but he softened his tone. "Kami, what's up?"

"Grey just got a call from the hospital. Ruby's waking up."

Alarms blared in his head. The doctors had been backing off the coma-inducing meds to give Ruby a chance to wake up, but the timing was too coincidental for him to like it. "Who did she talk to?"

"I don't know. I think she's in shock. Lana took her phone, but whoever called had already hung up."

Shit. "I'm five minutes away. Move to the safe room and keep an eye on her. I'll get verification on Ruby."

"Will do."

"One of you stay near the activation panel for the room, just in case."

"You got it." Kami had to be curious about what was going on, but she promised to act instead of peppering him with questions.

A quick call to Simon verified that Ruby was in fact waking. Her room was a steady flow of nurses and doctors checking her vitals and asking questions to see what she remembered.

"I had a few minutes with her before anyone came in," Simon said. "She's heard Grey's voice and remembers some of the conversations she's heard. For the sake of the hospital staff, I'm her fiancé and was out of town when she was first brought in."

"Good."

"Listen, I'm having them move her to a private room now that she's awake."

"Don't let her out of your sight."

"Not for a second."

Liam took the exit for his subdivision and ran options in his head. Ruby being awake was a good thing, but it complicated matters. The U.S. Marshals could sell her on the idea of protection, and Grey would follow. Ruby could slip and say something that would unknowingly endanger Grey, especially if she remembered everything they talked about in the room. The team could look at ways to move her someplace more secure, but a pending operation limited their options. So did cooperation with the U.S. Marshals.

Five minutes later Liam pulled into his garage and lowered the door.

He was entering the kitchen by the time the garage door bumped the concrete. The kitchen was a mess, with chocolate smears and drops all over the place. Rows of confections in varying shapes and sizes covered the counters. Liam got twitchy if he was in a dirty space too long, but he forced himself to ignore the mess they'd made and went across the hall to the safe room.

Few knew that a button press was all it would take to turn the media room into a sealed panic room comfortable enough to live in for several days. Lori stood at the entry, on guard. Kami and Lana sat on either side of Grey working to calm her.

"Tell me what you need, Liam," Lori said quietly.

"I'm going to take you up on that. In a minute." He touched her elbow in thanks and went to kneel before Grey.

She stared straight ahead. Unblinking. He got her to look at him long enough to assure himself she was okay before filling

Lana, Kami and Lori in on who Grey was, the trouble she was in and how their help was needed to lead any danger away.

Through it all, Grey sat and stared straight ahead. Unable to tell if she was paying attention or not, he moved closer to her side and refrained from mentioning Jessup by name. If Simon's guess was right, and it normally was, Jessup would already know Ruby was awake.

On board to help, Kami, Lana and Lori went out the front and got in their cars. Kami and Lori put their convertible tops up. Liam took Grey's hand and led her to the convertible he kept on hand for his family.

It was identical to Kami's, which would only help in their evasion. Anyone watching would expect Liam to leave in the 300. With the top and tinted windows up, Liam backed out. Lori went first, then Kami, then Liam and Lana took up the rear.

In the event someone had gotten close enough to watch the house and see them pulling out, they took the long way through the neighborhood and changed order a few times. When they exited the main gate, they split up and went different directions, giving Jessup, if he was already tracking Grey, a tougher target to tail.

Grey said nothing until Liam turned onto the highway, heading away from the hospital. "Aren't you taking me to see Ruby?"

"Yes. Just not directly."

"Why? What's going on? You're acting strange."

She'd moved blindly and silently wherever he guided her. The complacency wasn't like her and that disturbed him. If a phone call about Ruby shook her so badly, how eager would she be to snap up a new protection offer?

Willing to play any hand he thought would convince her to stay, Liam chose the one he thought would work best. Direct honesty. It would be tough to take, especially while she was still reeling from the news about Ruby, but he had to trust she could handle it.

"Jessup escaped."

Grey jerked. Her hand reached for the handle as if she was bracing for a quick escape.

Liam continued. "The U.S. Marshals, including Micah Carpenter, are in town. They're hunting Jessup and any of his connections. They'll also be looking for you so they can invite you back into protection."

"I can't leave Ruby."

"And they're not asking you to."

"They're willing to move her too?"

"Yes." His teeth clenched at how easily she grabbed on to the new offer when she'd shut down at the news of Ruby waking up. She didn't have to say she would entertain anything they offered. She wanted freedom and she wanted it with her sister. If she could have that...

"What about the donation?"

"The U.S. Marshals have been spinning stories and making people disappear for years. I'm sure they'd have that covered." He turned in to the office parking lot and pulled into the spot beside Aidan's car.

"Come on," he leaned over and opened her door before stepping out. Aidan exited his car, took Liam's keys and stood back for him to back out.

"Why are we playing all these car games if we're just heading to the hospital anyway? If Jessup is out and around, he's going to see me coming."

Liam reached into the backseat and grabbed a small bag. Grey reached in and pulled out a wig that would give her long, red hair with black-tipped bangs. A bottle of water and sponge would allow her to put a scar-looking tattoo on her face.

"You think this is going to be enough to throw Jessup off?"

"The more elaborate the disguise the easier it is to see through. Plus, Ruby is going to be moved to another floor. While Jessup may have someone in the hospital, he can't have the place as wired as we do."

"That's not going to stop Jessup from finding her, or me, if he's looking."

Grey was scared, and while it pissed Liam off to have to deliver the news, he was relieved to see that she appreciated the seriousness of the situation. "No, but it will limit their ability to monitor every movement in and around the room."

"So, is the plan to have me look like someone different every time I go in to see her, because that's going to be conspicuous."

"The plan right now is to get you to Ruby and stay as hidden as possible. I need you to play along. I need to know you and I are on the same page and that you'll do what I ask without questioning me."

"You don't want me to go back with Micah."

"No. I don't." He pulled into the parking garage of the hospital and found a spot in a shadowy corner near the stairs. Backing in, he stayed aware.

"What do you want, Liam? What do you want me to do?"

"I want to lock you up in the house and not let you out until Jessup is back behind bars or dead. I don't think you'll let me do that, though."

She shook her head and began finger combing the wig. When she slipped it on he smiled. "I like your short hair, but this look suits you."

"I had this hair for a couple of months in college." She smoothed her hand over the black tips and smiled. Then her eyes narrowed. "How'd you know these clothes might suit me?"

"I described the woman I know now and the one I met in Vegas to Kami. She did the rest. Though the skull-printed bra and underwear you stripped out of at the beach were pretty big hints." Now that she'd asked he took the time to consider the clothes she'd chosen that morning. The ripped shirt took four years off her age and teased him with thin flashes of skin. The jeans accentuated the small swell of her hips and hugged her narrow thighs and calves. The studded-toe flats polished off the edge.

"But you said this morning that something in the case should suit me."

"Kami has a way of knowing how to put people at ease. I trusted her to have the same skill with shopping."

Grey plucked at the shirt and sighed. "I still can't believe I'm wearing clothes Kami Evans picked out for me. Or that I spent the morning cooking with her."

Liam uncapped the water bottle and wetted the sponge. "You have a lot in common with her, you know."

"With Kami?"

"Yes." Leaning across the car, he placed the scar tattoo at the edge of Grey's nose so it ran along the curve of her smile line. Placing the sponge over the paper, he began applying the tattoo. "She had no training but she risked everything to prove her stepbrother didn't kill himself. She could have been killed if she hadn't trusted Breck. And the rest of us."

"Are you trying to say things will work out as well for me as they did for her?"

He brushed a dribble of water from her cheek with his thumb and pulled the sponge away. Slowly, he peeled the paper backing off the tattoo and supporting her chin with his fingers he studied the effect. The latex was a smidge darker than her skin tone and had a slightly bumpy texture. It looked like a genuine scar.

"I can't guarantee that."

"What can you guarantee?" she whispered. Her gaze moved over his face, struck him as borderline desperate.

He hadn't kissed her yet for the day, and had planned on waiting until they had more time alone. In the shadowy confines of Aidan's car, with Grey asking for guarantees, the need to show her instead of tell her swelled.

Applying the lightest pressure on his fingers, he pulled her face closer. Leaving himself open for a better kiss later, he pressed his lips to the scar he'd just given her. "That I will do everything possible to keep you and Ruby safe. If that means I have to scrub up to stand guard in the operating room then I will."

"The doctors won't allow that."

"If I have your permission and Director Quinn's backing we can find a way to make it happen."

He pressed his lips to the corner of hers and breathed her in. She smelled of chocolate and sugar and his body melted beneath the desire to devour. "I'll do anything necessary if it means you're safe."

"Would you go into WitSec with me?"

He pulled back and met her gaze. Leaving his family and friends would rip a hole in his heart and soul, but so had being without Grey since meeting her. Being worried she was in danger had filled him with fear. If she went without him he would always wonder and worry.

"If you asked." Because if she asked him to go it would mean she thought they could have something. He would risk most anything for a chance at what his parents had shared for years.

"Really? Why?"

He only smiled and whispered, "This doesn't count." Then he laid his mouth directly over hers and kissed her. She raised a hand and curled her fingers around his neck. The tips pressed gently into his skin. Her lips opened on a sigh and Liam almost took advantage of the opportunity.

She arched her back and released a tiny moan. It took all his restraint to keep from climbing into her seat with her, laying her back and indulging. He kept the kiss light though, with only a hint of hunger until she pulled back. When she did, she was quietly panting.

"Liam."

"I want you, Grey." He pressed another kiss to her lips, but didn't linger. "As much as I want you safe I want to know where we could take this thing between us."

"So you would follow me?"

"Yes."

"I'd feel bad for taking you away from your family."

"You're my family too." *And I love you.*

The words wanted to tumble free. He wanted her to be ready to hear them, but his wants weren't the important ones. Only Grey's mattered.

"It can't be that simple for you."

He shrugged. "It can, but right now you should focus on Ruby." He kissed her once more. "You've waited long enough for this."

Chapter Fourteen

Liam hadn't immediately said he would go with her into WitSec, but he'd said he would. His reason had been scarier than the agreement.

You're my family too.

Thinking too much about his answer, when an offer hadn't officially been made by the U.S. Marshals, was a waste of energy, so Grey turned her attention to their mission of the moment. "What's the next part of your plan? I'm guessing you're trying to get me unseen into Ruby's room. Tell me what to do."

"You make keeping you safe easy, Grey."

"Only because I'm getting my way."

"I think you're just glad for a break from hiding everything." He tilted his head sideways while shrugging with his eyebrows. "But I'll take what I can get."

He leaned across her, as he had every time they'd exited a car together, and opened her door. When they met at the hood, he placed a hand on her back and guided her toward the door.

"We're going in through the professional building since Jessup or his people will most likely expect to see you come in through one of the main entrances. When we pass people, you'll feel like you need to duck your head and hide your face."

That had been exactly how she'd felt every time they'd entered the hospital. "If they can't see my face they can't identify me."

"True. But hiding your face can actually draw more attention, and if you're looking away you can't identify them. If you can look people in the eye you'll be able to convince them you're not afraid."

"And if I am?"

"Then you fake the bravery until it's no longer necessary."

She glanced up at Liam. He was looking directly into her eyes, and it occurred to her that he was always looking up and directly at people. The warmth in his gaze had always pulled her in and had her trying to figure out what he was thinking. It had never occurred to her to avoid his gaze, just as it had never occurred to her that looking directly at people was likely something he'd learned rather than something he did naturally.

Or was it? Maybe it was something some people were just better at than others.

She'd looked down and away when she'd shared the elevator with Jessup's man. Thinking back, she'd looked down and away when Jessup had found her in the storage room. In fact, she'd never looked him in the eyes.

"You can do this, Grey."

Liam opened the door that led into the professional building. Meeting his gaze was easy, but she was suddenly aware of her discomfort with meeting peoples' gazes. A wig and fake scar didn't really help. "I think I'd rather be in hiding."

"Listen." Liam pulled her to a stop. "There's every chance Micah will show up pretty quick to offer you protection."

"So you've said."

"And I'll go with you if you want."

She smiled, but didn't feel happy about it.

"Can I offer you an alternative?"

Please. She nodded.

"Stay here. Trust my team, trust me, to keep you and Ruby safe. We'll get the operation done as soon as they clear you, and then we'll move you both to my house as soon as possible."

"There's a hospital stay of up to seven days after a kidney surgery."

"I know. We'll get registered nurses to stay at the house to help you both. You will be safe with us. With me."

"Not that I mind the idea of not being in a hospital, but wouldn't it be easier for you to catch Jessup if Ruby and I are here?"

"There's nothing easy about you being in danger." He took her hand in his big one, linked her fingers with his long ones and led her downstairs. "Besides, at home we have better control over the people in and out of your rooms."

"You seem confident this is all going to work out." His outlook was appealing and something she normally would have led with. "I would've pegged you for a glass half empty kind of guy."

"And I had you pegged as a glass half full gal." He opened the stairwell door, scanning the area before he opened it wide enough for her to pass. He was on high alert as they walked purposefully through the lobby.

"I used to be." Grey worked at keeping her chin up and meeting the eyes of anyone she saw looking at her.

"You still are. This just matters more than anything else."

Grey thought about *this* and all the ways he could mean it as they turned down a hall that led through the back of the hospital. They were well away from the main entrance as he opened another stairwell door.

He never hesitated to read a sign, but instead moved like he knew exactly where he was going and belonged everywhere. "When did you study the layout of this place, Liam?"

"When I was watching Ruby sleep and waiting for you to arrive."

"Did you know then we'd need these back paths?"

He shrugged. "It's never bad to be prepared. And Tyler makes it easy for us."

At the door to the third floor, he held up a finger for her to wait. She stepped away from the door, pressed her back to the wall. He opened the door and looked up and down the hall. He muttered a curse, but offered a hand.

Whatever he'd seen it wasn't something to hide her from. When she cleared the door, she understood. Marshal Micah Carpenter stood a few doors down talking to two suited men.

Micah looked up and his gaze bored directly into Grey as if the large man at her side was invisible. Or didn't exist. Knowing Micah, he'd prefer the non-existence angle.

"Greycen." Micah's tone was brusque as he cut through the two men he'd been talking to and headed her way. He moved like he spoke, always focused on the target. In five years she'd never seen him laugh or even smile a smile that reached his eyes. And though she'd trusted him, she'd never really liked him.

"Micah."

"You haven't checked in. We need to talk." He reached for her elbow, something else she noticed he always did. He never gave her the chance to argue.

"No." She shifted her shoulder back, pulling just out of his reach. "I need to see Ruby."

"Your sister is fine. She's going to be entering the program."

Grey lifted her eyebrows and, taking Liam's advice, met Micah's gaze directly. "Has she signed your contracts?"

He narrowed his eyes, a move more telling than his head shake. He hadn't won yet. Stepping around him, empowered by Liam's presence, she moved toward Ruby's room. "You can't go in there," Micah said.

Grey turned. Liam stepped in front of her and stopped Micah. "Neither Grey nor Ruby are your jurisdiction, but they are under my protection. You're going to want to back off."

"It's only a matter of time, Agent Burgess, before you lose her again."

Liam vibrated. Visibly. Grey rested her hand on his back and left it there as she stepped up to stand beside him. "What are you saying, Micah?"

He looked stunned, but recovered quickly. "Karl Jessup is dangerous."

"So are you, Liam and his team. I'm safe."

The only time she'd disagreed or argued with Micah had been when she left Vegas to see Ruby. She'd done that over the phone, because she'd known she would bow to the force of his convictions if she faced him. She'd learned something since leaving, though, mainly from Kami and Lori. Life could kick her teeth down her throat, but she could get through it with the right support system.

"Liam and I are going in to see Ruby. I'll let you know if I want to discuss an offer of protection."

Micah pointed at Liam, but didn't look away from Grey. "Did he tell you about Jessup?"

"That he's escaped? Yes. That he's gunning for me?" Her fingers went to the scratches on her face. "I'm well aware."

"His hired gun is in this hospital, and there's likely more than one."

"His hired gun, as you call the guy, is in a hospital bed under guard." She rested a hand on Liam's arm and smiled. "Mine isn't."

She said nothing else as she turned and closed the distance to Ruby's room. Like Micah had cut through the two men standing nearby, so did she. The whole way, Liam was silent at her back.

Grey had waited long enough to see her sister again. Despite the worry about the tension between them when she left, she pushed the room door open and went in without delay.

The head of Ruby's bed had been raised so she was sitting up. Simon sat on the edge of the narrow mattress, saying something that had Ruby smiling. He stopped when she turned her head on the pillow and looked at Grey. Her smile wobbled but then widened.

A welcome rain after a draught, tears fell from Grey's eyes as she crossed the room in a rush. Simon stood and backed away. Grey, careful not to bump a bruise or cast, wrapped her arms around her sister and hugged her.

Ruby's good arm came around her and squeezed her close. They didn't speak. There was a lot to be said, but for the moment words were less important than the confirmation of their connection.

Two years older, Ruby had been seventeen when their parents had walked away. She'd been awarded emancipation and then had fought for custody of Grey. Every meal had been a struggle, but they'd had each other. When Grey hit rock bottom, unable to cope, Ruby had been there. When she sank a second time, Ruby had still been there.

"I'm sorry, Ruby. I'm sorry about everything." She'd left thinking she was protecting Ruby for a change. She'd thought wrong. "I was screwed up, but I shouldn't have left."

"It's okay." Ruby brushed her hand down the length of Grey's hair, the wig, the way she had so many times before. "I'm pretty well caught up. You did the right thing when you left, which makes me prouder than you can know, but I'm glad you're back."

Grey eased back and took Ruby's uninjured hand in hers. "They want to take me back into WitSec."

"I know. They offered me protection."

Grey looked behind her to where Liam and Simon leaned against the wall. Both men had their arms crossed as they watched her and Ruby in silence. Grey considered asking them to leave her and Ruby alone. She was pretty sure Liam would honor her request, but then she met his gaze.

He would leave the room and let her talk to Ruby privately. He'd do anything she asked. Knowing that, she needed no other reason to trust him. She'd called him her hired gun, but he was so much more.

Certain she was making the right decision, Grey turned back to Ruby. "You may have noticed you've been sleeping with round-the-clock guard dogs."

"And an apparent fiancé." Ruby looked past her and smiled at Simon. "Yeah."

"If it's okay with you," Grey spoke to Ruby, but she turned and met Liam's gaze, "I'd like to leave things in their hands."

Liam's mouth lifted into one of his rare smiles. He tilted his head with the tiniest acknowledgement. They were nowhere close to having things settled between them, but with him and Simon—Ruby's undercover fiancé it seemed—and everyone else at her back she only needed the U.S. Marshals to track Jessup.

Ruby nodded toward Liam and asked, "You trust him?"

"I do. So, if you're okay with keeping your own identity and life, I say we reject Marshal Carpenter's offer." Grey's answer was automatic and without a shred of doubt. She'd trusted Micah to keep her safe, but her loyalty ended there. With Liam... Given enough time she could trust him with everything.

Liam uncrossed his arms and stepped forward. He didn't cross all the way to her, though, and his eyes held an uncertainty she wouldn't have thought him capable of. "Are you sure, Grey?"

"If Ruby's on board, yes."

"I've been asleep the entire time they've been in my life," Ruby said. "If you trust them I see no reason I shouldn't."

More tears burned Grey's eyes. Ruby's easy acceptance and faith was more than she deserved. She would do everything to make sure it was the right choice. "Then we're staying."

Liam sighed an exhalation that carried the cloud of doubt from his eyes. He'd been willing to give up his life, but was clearly relieved it wouldn't come to that. Having spent the last five years without her sister, Grey knew exactly what misery he was avoiding. Glad she could do something for him for a change, she smiled. Maybe it would help make up for walking out on him.

A knock on the door broke off any more conversation. Simon checked it and when he opened it all the way it was to admit Dr. Keiths. Silver hair and wrinkly eyes were the main signs of age. The doctor was tall and fit and carried himself with the confidence of a successful surgeon.

"Ms. Donovan." He smiled at Ruby. "It's great to see you awake." He turned his smile on Grey. It was more of a practiced smile than a genuine one, but she'd seen worse when she'd met with him for the donor screening appointments. "Grey?" The doctor hesitated only briefly over her new look. "I didn't expect to see you here."

"I heard she was awake and couldn't stay away." Grey tried to smile, but couldn't pull it off. Her stomach rolled with the possibilities of news he could be bringing. If she wasn't a match or if they couldn't find a donor or if there were other complications that only showed up after Ruby woke... The list was endless and increasingly torturous.

"Dr. Keiths." Liam saved her from her thoughts. "How's Ruby doing?"

"Her vitals are strong." Dr. Keiths moved to the side of the bed opposite of Grey and looked at Ruby's chart he'd carried in. "Aside from needing a new kidney she's healing."

"Any news on a transplant?" Simon asked, playing the part of devoted fiancé.

"Ms. Craig here has applied to be a living donor," Dr. Keiths said with a nod toward Grey. "We're waiting for the results on one last test, but so far everything looks good."

Grey's heart fluttered. "You mean I should be able to donate?"

"We'll know for certain by end of day, but it's looking that way."

"When would we be able to do the surgery?" Grey asked.

"Once we get the final approval we'll have some paperwork to process and then should be able to move forward." Dr. Keiths patted her bicep. "With any luck, tomorrow or the next day."

"Seriously?" she squeaked. She hadn't squeaked in... She couldn't remember the last time she'd squeaked. Giddy with happiness, Grey turned to Ruby. "This is awesome. You could have a new kidney and be out of here in just over a week."

Ruby wasn't smiling at the news. She still wasn't smiling when Dr. Keiths left the room a few minutes later. He was thrilled to see Ruby awake and talking, but he was concerned by her color—she was too pale. And her energy—she could only turn her head on the pillow.

"Don't you want out of here, Ruby? Don't you want to be better?"

"Of course. I just don't want you to be my donor. You have enough to deal with."

"If you were really listening while in your coma, you'd know you're the reason I'm back." Grey lifted her sister's hand and squeezed it gently. "The surgery isn't a big deal."

"You can't protect yourself during a surgery or recovery."

"You're right," Liam said, stepping forward. "And you can't take care of yourself until you get a new kidney." He pointed between Simon and himself. "Protection is why we're here. And why the rest of my team will be here when we can't be."

"If she risks herself and things go wrong—"

"That's not going to happen," Liam cut in harshly.

"—she wouldn't be able to testify."

The line in Liam's forehead cratered, his mouth hardened. "She will testify, because nothing is happening to her."

"She's right here," Grey stated. "Ruby, you sacrificed so much for me when we were younger." A college education. A relationship. "Let me do this for you."

Ruby argued, but it didn't hold much fire. "You were always too impetuous."

"I assure you I've considered the angles." Even if something did go wrong in the surgery, not that she wanted to think it would, Liam and his team were gathering enough evidence to put Jessup away when he was caught again. And if she needed to, she would do a video statement. A good defense attorney could get it dismissed, probably, but if a jury got to see it they'd be hard pressed to forget what she'd have to say.

"Ruby." Simon circled Ruby's bed and sat on the edge of it. "I've seen a lot of families torn apart by life. Some are lucky enough to find each other again. Others die before getting the chance."

"Cheery thought," Ruby muttered.

"You're in a hospital with an amazing success rate. You have one of the FBI's top teams and the U.S. Marshals Service at your back. This thing Grey wants to do for you, it's such a small thing when you consider the likely reward."

Ruby turned to Simon. "What do you think that would be?"

He smiled a quiet smile that spoke of simplicity. His answer, one whispered word, moved through Grey like a promise and brought tears to her eyes. "Life."

Ruby narrowed her eyes and scowled. "You're really good at that guilt game."

"Guilt would be telling you I'd like you to live long enough to get to know you." Simon bent down and kissed her temple. "If you're going to deny Grey's offer, make sure you have a reason other than fear."

Grey didn't argue her case further. Nothing she added would be more convincing than Simon. At least she hoped he was convincing, because she suddenly felt more lost than Mulan in a man's army. Ruby was her Shang, the one person she needed to convince but the one who wouldn't listen because of whom she was. Or whom she'd been.

Chapter Fifteen

Exhaustion grew nearer with every mile closer to home, but Liam forced his mind to stay sharp. He watched for any sign of a tail, but found none. He scanned the area around his neighborhood for indications of danger, but saw none.

When he pulled into his garage and lowered the door, he finally relaxed. Resting his head against the seat, he turned and looked at Grey. Her eyes were closed and her chest rose and fell in a steady rhythm. Her face muscles twitched too much for her to be completely relaxed in sleep though.

"You're awfully quiet, Grey." And it was awful, because unlike the other silences they'd shared her fear and worry moved through this one. And him. The more concerned she became the more energy it took for him to fight it.

She didn't open her eyes, but her face stilled. Her throat moved in a swallow and her fragility had Liam gripping the steering wheel to keep from pulling her to him. He hadn't kissed her yet today, except the brief teaser after hearing Jessup escaped, and the idea of pulling her into his lap had the temptation snapping to the forefront.

Flowing a little quicker and smoother through his veins, his blood heated.

"Just thinking." As if it had been hours since she'd spoken, her voice was thick and raspy. It hadn't been hours, though, so it had to be a product of emotion.

"Are you having doubts about tomorrow?"

Her head rolled from side to side on the seat. "Not a one. I know I'm doing the right thing with the donation."

Needing to touch her, to reassure himself if not her, he took her hand in his. Rubbing his thumb over her fingers he studied the contrast of her softness against his calloused fingers. In the big picture of life they barely knew each other, but he knew everything about her he needed to know.

He'd seen the depths of her kindness and loyalty. She made him feel stronger just by being near. He was miserable without her. He'd even painted his walls gray because the color made him think of her—not that he was admitting that to anyone.

"Wanna tell me what you're thinking about?"

With her face toward him, she breathed deep and opened her eyes. Quiet certainty penetrated the shield of her contacts. The same certainty whispered in her one word answer. "You."

Hearts shouldn't stop and chests shouldn't collapse, but his did. A beat later his heart kicked into action with a new life and his chest opened up to make room. It was a struggle, but he kept his voice light. "Really?"

"Since walking into Ruby's room and finding you in that chair, I've been waiting for you to turn into an impatient asshole, but you haven't."

"That almost sounded like a compliment."

She smiled softly and the look seemed to be reflected deep in her soul. "You had every reason to hate me, but you've been supporting me since before I got back."

He shrugged and continued playing with her fingers.

"You sat with my sister and protected her. You've kept me safe even when I didn't want you to."

"I care about you, Grey."

"I've given you multiple reasons to want to yell at me, but you haven't."

"Yelling would only make you feel bad, which would then make me feel bad for making you feel bad."

She laughed. "I'm pretty sure that's what has me falling for you."

He grinned, raised his gaze to hers. His heart swelled. His eyes burned, but he refused to allow tears to fall. "I'm not going to apologize for that."

"I'm pretty sure that when I fall in love with you, and I'm thinking that's seriously possible, it will be forever."

"I'm sure as shit not going to apologize for *that*."

She laughed again and this time it stained her cheeks with a happy blush. "Of course not. But can I ask you to do something?"

"Anything." It came out as a sighing whisper, but the promise of it echoed inside him like a yodel.

"Take me to bed, Liam. Make love to me."

Everything stilled. His heart. Their breathing. The air moving around them. It all...stopped. Somewhere between Earth and Heaven miracles occurred. At the moment, that place was his garage and the granter was Grey.

Wordlessly, he opened his door and went around to open hers. Taking her hand, he waited for her to get to her feet. Then, he did something he'd wanted to do for two years. He swept Greycen Craig Burgess into his arms and carried her across the threshold into the house he'd dreamed of sharing with her.

"I can walk."

"You can, but you're not going to."

Her breath was warm against his neck as she rested her forehead against his temple. The arousal he'd managed not to think too much about the last few days snapped at its leash.

Liam didn't bother with lights as he headed to the bedroom, but once he stepped into his room, he hit the nearest switch. He wasn't going to miss a look or a breath or a reaction. If she only gave him tonight, he would memorize every instance.

He set her on her feet beside the bed and despite the ravaging hunger roaring inside, he brushed the tips of his fingers over her cheeks and over her fake scar. Her breath rushed for freedom. Two years had passed since he felt a woman's touch. Since he felt his wife's touch. Every moment of suffering became worthwhile when she smiled up at him and toed off the metallic silver Toms.

He curled a strand of her wig around his finger and tugged gently. "Are you sure about this, Grey?"

"I am, but could you do me another favor since there's no one else around?"

"Of course." Like the *anything* in the car, it came out as a whisper. He was powerless against her requests, and he didn't want to change it.

"Call me Opal. I think I miss being Opal."

His heart broke for all that she'd given up, but in the next moment it soared because she was empowering herself to take it all back. And *that* was *so* sexy.

"I always liked opals." He bent down and kissed her temple while simultaneously giving the wig a yank.

Opal gasped and reached for his shirt. She pulled it from his jeans.

"Are you sure you're sure about this?"

"Very." Proving her claim with action, she shoved his jacket off his shoulders and then, as if she'd done it before and so often it was natural, she unholstered his weapon.

He tensed for a flash. No one else handled his gun. Ever. But she carefully placed it on the bedside table so the handle was toward the bed, just as he did each night, and then turned her attention back to him.

"Are you sure about this, Liam?"

Fuck yeah. He rubbed his hands down her arms. "I've never been so sure, Opal."

She breathed deep, her eyes drifting closed. He took advantage of her momentarily dropped guard and swooped in. Two years of abstinence topped with days of restraint imploded his control.

His lips closed over hers, moved in a hungry pace she matched instantly. She clawed at his shirt and belt. He kicked off his shoes. When she reached for the snap of his pants, he jerked from desire's daze and grabbed her hands.

"I thought you were sure."

"I am. I'm also sure you're not going to attack me." He kissed her gently. "This time anyway."

She rolled her eyes but her hands slowed as they moved over his now naked torso. Her nails teased his nipples, leaving him to wonder if he'd miscalculated. Opal read his doubt if her grin was any indication.

"As I recall, attacking you holds a certain appeal."

Yeah, she'd read him correctly. She'd thought he was following her in Vegas, had slipped into a building's shadow and attacked him, demanded answers, when he passed. He'd answered her questions and then demanded she have dinner with him. That night had been the first time they'd slept together.

"Not this time." He grinned at the memory though as he lifted her shirt over her head. Liam checked his watch by twisting his wrist and leaning left a little. "I've waited, dreamed, of this far too long to rush it."

Liam knelt before her and kissed a path along the bottom edge of her bra. She was trembling when he made a return trip along the top edge of her pants. "Did I tell you," he began as he popped the top snap of her pants, "how much I like this look on you?"

She shook her head and shifted her stance, rubbing her thighs together.

"All day I've had glimpses of your skin and been teased by the edginess and tightness of these pants." He lowered the zipper and placed a nibbling and lingering kiss at her belly button. Ticklish where a small scar marred her smooth skin, her stomach twitched. "I've ached with the desire to peel away every layer of fabric hiding you."

"You seemed so unaffected."

"Grey. Opal." Still kneeling before her, he looked up. If she'd managed to touch a little lower when she'd reached for his pants she'd have known the truth. He got a certain pleasure from pointing it out. "I am never unaffected when you're near."

Her hands framed his head. She rolled her hips, moving her pussy closer to his mouth. "Then, please, hurry up and show me."

As weightless as an eagle in flight, Liam undressed the woman he'd promised his life to. Every inch of exposed skin was a dream realized and then the ultimate fantasy became reality. Opal stood naked in his bedroom.

"How's it possible that you've gotten more beautiful?"

169

"Absence has made you delusional."

"I'm not." Determined to prove himself, Liam flipped back the bed covers, picked her up and then laid her down. Stripping away his remaining clothes, he joined her on the bed. Hands and mouth, brushing touches and breathy kisses, he explored her body until she writhed beneath him.

"Liam. Please."

Gooseflesh popped up on her skin and his. Fiery passion and calculated restraint battled within.

His body's needs became a command that needed to be obeyed, but he had an insight into Grey, Opal, he'd lacked before. She needed to know she was cherished, whatever name she chose, as much as he needed her to understand *he* was the one who cherished her.

Patience grew from adoration. Liam covered her in a trail of kisses that went down to her toes and left them both trembling. He was beginning his way back when she lunged, flipped him to his back and straddled him.

"You're taking too long."

She cocked her head and rubbed her wet sex along the length of his erection. Damn if he didn't nearly lose it.

"I've waited two years to have you in this bed." He flipped her so she was on her back. Like she had, he cocked his head and rubbed himself against her. She bucked, but he pulled away before she could achieve her goal. "I'm taking my time with you."

Grey moved to flip him again. Liam resisted her attempt by stiffening. "In Vegas, you let me be on top."

"In Vegas—" he kissed her hip bone while dancing his fingers down her side, "—I had every reason to believe we'd be together more often."

"I've promised not to leave without talking to you." She rested a hand against his face. He leaned into the touch, but his fingers stayed busy, edged closer to her pussy.

"Yep. And you're about to have a surgery that's going to keep you in a hospital bed for at least a week." He traced the edge of her nether lips. Her hips bucked again. "I'm making sure you have plenty to think about."

Locking his gaze with hers so she could see everything he felt, Liam eased a finger inside. She was wet and tight and so warm. He wanted to pull out and then sink deep so she circled his dick.

He slipped a second finger in with the first and thumbed her clit. His balls tightened and pulled up inside his body. Pressure built in his abdomen and lower back.

"Liam." Her cry of desperation shook the room and put a smile on his heart.

He rotated his fingers, pushed deeper, pulled out. She fisted the covers, dug her head into the pillow and arched off the mattress. Her orgasm was close and as much fun as it was to go over with her, this time was all about her.

The nub of her clit hardened beneath the sweeping touch of his thumb. She swelled around his fingers and pulsed with the rapidly approaching orgasm. Her breath came in little pants, each one a balm to the wounds on his heart.

Everything he remembered about their time together had been spot on. The years of searching for her, planning a home for her, dreaming of her, were paying off with new memories. One day, when she was safe, he'd capture some memories with a camera, but for now his mind would have to be enough.

Ready to nudge her over the edge, Liam leaned forward and kissed her. Still moving against his fingers with beads of sweat dotting her hair line, she dove into the kiss.

She placed her hands on his hips and eased them forward, toward his dick. Her fingers wrapped him, squeezed and pumped. Her hips bucked, bumping his hand against hers. The pressure in his back and abdomen built. She was going to force him to join her, but he didn't want to miss the sensation of her clenching around him.

Pulling away quickly, he sat back, panting. "You're going to kill me."

"The solution is a simple one." The smile curling her lips penetrated her eyes and brightened the room. It was a happy one. Happy and unreserved.

Pulled in by the brilliance, he reached over her and opened the drawer beside the bed.

"We don't need a condom."

"Sure we do."

She shook her head. "I trust that you're clean. And pregnancy isn't going to be an issue."

That last statement required a conversation, because every quivering instinct told him it wasn't a matter of her birth control choices. Those same instincts told him that pulling away would shatter what they were building.

He moved back, bracing his hands on either side of her shoulders. "I'm clean."

"Me too." As if she'd just won a major victory, she lifted her legs and wrapped them around his waist. Using the leverage of the grip, she pulled her hips up and slipped onto his erection.

Her sigh was a shudder and it moved into him, eliciting a gasp. Hot, wet, tight. She closed around him, body against body with no barrier. The sensations fired in rapid succession, fueling another round. Then she set her hands on his hips, dug the tips of her fingers into him and began to move.

Thoughts and control vacated. His body took over and joined her in the climb. Quick and then slow, slow and then fast, he alternated the speed of thrusts and withdrawals. He breathed deep, drew her scent into his lungs and absorbed the feel of her touch as they plummeted over the edge to release.

In the quiet afterglow, Liam brushed a hand over her short hair. "Sex aside, I'm glad you're back, Opal."

His wife was brave, smart and daring. She made him smile when he didn't think he could. She woke him body and soul with a caress and slayed him with a request.

She'd asked him to make love to her. It had been a partnership from the beginning, and not because they were good in bed. Their partnership had started when they exchanged vows, but even in separation, with each of them honoring those vows, they'd continually reaffirmed their connection.

She would have her surgery, help Ruby. They would both recover. Jessup would be caught. Then, in the lull of safety, he would ask her to stay. If what they'd just shared was an accurate indicator, he wouldn't have to worry about rejection.

Chapter Sixteen

Liam's heartbeat was strong and steady beneath Grey's ear. A sunset's silence surrounded the house. Tomorrow's surgery loomed, which should worry her, but for the first time in years, she felt completely free. More free even than she'd felt on the beach. "I've come to a decision."

"What's that?" Liam's Scottish accent became more defined when he neared sleep.

She'd allowed herself to forget that after walking away from him. Now she realized how much she'd missed it.

"When this is all over—the surgery, Jessup, everything—I don't want to give up the identity the U.S. Marshal Service gave me."

"Why's that?" His fingers combed through her hair, tickling the nape of her neck at the end of each swipe. She snuggled deeper into his side.

"Hearing you call me Opal. It wasn't right. Opal's dead."

"She's not dead. She's just changed."

"No. When I chose those torn clothes I was clinging to who I was. I wanted to be Opal, because she was free and daring and didn't care what people thought of her. She did what she wanted, when she wanted, damn the consequences."

"Sounds a little like the woman I married."

"Undeniably so." She traced the contours of his chest and stomach, soaking in the luxuriousness of the moment. "But the woman you married prefers the idea of a tight circle of friends instead of a large circle of acquaintances. She doesn't dress in ways that draw attention to herself. She wants nothing more than to be a part of something special." Tears crowded her eyes. "And she wants to have children. Opal didn't care about any of that."

"Grey's your legal name, so if that's the one you prefer it's easy to keep. As for the things you want, you can have them. Some of them you already have."

She shook her head against him. He'd chased away nightmares and welcomed her into his home, arms and family. She was safe with him. Her secrets had to be too. "Remember when I said a condom wasn't necessary?"

"I do."

"That's because I can't have kids."

"Do you want to tell me why?" His question was soft and held zero judgment.

She'd talked it out in therapy enough that the words were easy. Having the confidence he'd feel the same way about her when he heard her story was another.

He would hear it sooner or later. Now was better than in a courtroom during a trial. At least now she had the benefit of not looking him in the face to see his pity. "Ruby had just turned seventeen when our parents walked out on us. She got the courts to give her custody of me, but I didn't take the abandonment well."

"Few would."

"I began experimenting with drugs, alcohol and sex. Ruby was so busy working and trying to keep us fed and housed that I got away with it for a long while. Until I got arrested for stealing some chips from a convenience store."

"I found that police report when I connected you to Ruby," he whispered, like it was a secret he shouldn't tell. What he knew barely cracked the surface of her scab-covered past.

"Ruby bailed me out and got me cleaned up. She helped me get my grades turned around in time to apply for college. Fast forward to my first round of semester finals. The pressure got to me and I started using again. Ruby tried to get me clean, but I wouldn't listen. She took the hard line and told me to call her when I was ready to stop using."

"You were still using when you witnessed the Matoots' murders."

She moved her head in a nod. "I was easing off. I hadn't talked to Ruby in nearly a year, and had almost thought I was strong enough to reach out again."

"She still loves you, Grey. I can tell by watching you two together that she's never stopped."

"Yeah, but there was a time when I didn't love her. Or, I loved the drugs more."

"You're not the first person to have an addiction, but you got clean." He turned her to face him. "And you became a stronger person because of it."

"I'm not strong."

"More than you know, but you'll have to see it for yourself." He brushed a thumb over her eyebrow. The kindness in his brown eyes encouraged her. "Tell me the rest."

"They were smuggling drugs in cake mixes sold locally. A package went missing and a kid overdosed." She swallowed and forced herself not to look away. "I took it. "I gave him the pills. We split them.

"A kid died because of me, which made the Matoots change their minds, which is why they confronted Jessup." Her heart rate sped. The dream would be particularly vivid tonight, as it always was when she thought about the night her life came to an end. "They died because of me and then I snapped up the U.S. Marshals' offer so no one could find out what I'd done. In the process, I left my sister behind, never giving her the truth she deserved."

Liam didn't look at her with judgment or pity. In fact, he looked at her no differently than he had since meeting her. With kindness and understanding.

"That night." She braced herself for the next part. She didn't remember all of it, dissociative amnesia a doctor had called it, but what she did recall had to be said. "Jessup found me hiding in the storeroom. The only other employee was a new mom who was definitely too good to touch a drug. He knew I was the one who'd taken his product. He'd just lost a profitable distribution avenue."

"He was pissed," Liam said.

"I expected him to pull his gun and end it as quickly as he had for them." Her stomach knotted. "He said he wanted me to suffer. He stabbed me multiple times."

It was the first time she'd said it without shuddering and it was because of Liam.

Liam ran a finger over the scar by her belly button. "He did this to you?"

She nodded. "And then, while I was bleeding all over the place, he raped me."

"How did you get away? How did you survive?"

"I remember hearing someone outside the storeroom, but it goes black after that. The next thing I remember, I was in the hospital with Micah passing me a contract and promising to keep me safe."

Liam was silent for a long time. His finger moved back and forth over the scar he'd kissed earlier. "You can't have children because of the attack."

She shook her head.

"And you want them."

"It's something I've thought a little about." Primarily in the last two years after having glimpsed married life with a man who seemed like he'd be a good father.

"There are alternatives."

"Not for a woman in WitSec or for one with my past." She had screwed up too badly to deserve a child. She had too far to go for redemption.

"Grey..." Liam's phone rang. "Shit."

He reached for it and looked at the display. His brows drew together in that way that enhanced the vertical line. Pressing Talk, he raised the phone. "Micah."

Grey tried to hear what Micah said, but he was too muffled by the phone against Liam's ear. Liam smiled in a way that encouraged her, but what really lifted her spirit was the way he reached out and straightened her hair.

"Ten minutes will be fine."

Liam ended the call and dropped the phone on the bed. He looked around with his shoulders slumped.

"What is it?"

"Micah's heading over with an attorney to get your video statement."

"Oh." She'd forgotten all about Micah and the statement, and for the first time she didn't like the idea of her time with Liam being interrupted. "I guess we should get dressed."

Liam called the guard on duty and the front gate to approve Micah and the attorney for entry.

They got out of bed, neither moving quickly, both giving the other brushing touches as they passed each other their clothes and got dressed.

With phones in their pockets and his gun again holstered on his belt they headed for the door. He took her hand and pulled her to a stop. She looked up at him. For a moment he said nothing, just looked at her.

With a sigh, he brushed a finger along her cheek. Whatever he might have said went unspoken as he instead leaned in and kissed her. With the fingers of one hand linked with hers and the fingers of his other hand resting on her cheek, the caress was tender and sweet. Raw in its intensity. Powerful in its ability to make her want to explore the alternatives with him.

Damn. She wanted to explore every moment of every day with him.

The doorbell peeled through the house. He pulled back and led her downstairs. Five minutes later, Micah and Grey were set up in the formal living room. The attorney, Micah said, was minutes away.

Micah's phone chimed at the same moment a light tapping sound came from the kitchen. Liam tensed and exchanged a look with Micah.

"Watch her. I'll check it."

Grey was on her feet and crossing to Liam before she could stop herself. Preparing to record her statement, a precaution in case something went wrong on the operating table, made the moment all too real. She didn't want to be apart from Liam for even a minute. "Do you...?"

"Yes." He smiled, as if he knew what she was feeling and shared the sentiment. Pulling her aside, he winked so only she saw it. His voice, when he spoke was a whisper. "If you aren't safe in this room with the man who's protected you for five years we have more issues than Karl Jessup."

"You're right." Micah was rarely the kindest person. More often than not he forgot people had feelings or opinions different from his own, but he wasn't a bad person.

The tapping came again, but this time was followed by the distinct sound of breaking glass. "I'll be right back," Liam promised.

She stiffened her spine and tried not to worry about whatever they'd heard. When she turned to return to her seat, Micah had unholstered his weapon and held it at his side.

So much for not worrying.

"You're sleeping with him." Micah shook his head and practically sneered.

"You're here for a case. You have no right to the details of my life any longer."

"I warned you you'd regret coming back here." He rotated his wrist at his side, rotating the gun.

Chills crawled across her skin. Moving closer to the entryway, she listened for Liam. She heard nothing. With fear at her back and suspicion in front of her, she eased her way into the foyer. Micah followed.

"Why exactly is that, Micah?" She fought to keep panic from her voice. She didn't know where Liam was or what he'd found and she didn't know exactly why she suddenly felt the need to be away from Micah, but she couldn't sit calmly in the living room and wait.

Step by careful step she worked her way through the foyer and down the hall toward the kitchen. Toward the safe room. Toward, she hoped, Liam.

"Are you really going to pretend you didn't feel something for me?"

She angled her head, shocked. What could she have possibly done to make him think...? It didn't matter. "I've considered you a friend, Micah."

"Friends who shared dinner regularly on Friday nights and weekend morning coffees."

All of which were under the guise of him checking up on her. She cocked her head and kept moving backward. Shuffling sounds and grunts reached her from the kitchen. Whatever was happening, she was on her own with Micah for a few more minutes.

"You wanted more."

He shrugged and continued rotating his wrist. "You're not like other women, Grey."

"If you wanted me for yourself, why would you call Liam? Why call the FBI if you wanted me back with you?"

"I needed to have eyes here in case Jessup made a move. Agent Burgess had checked into you. He seemed logical."

"Because you couldn't ask your own people to watch out for me?"

"You weren't in the program. I couldn't use our resources for you."

He spoke the truth, but there was more he wasn't saying. Something that had to do with the gun in his hand. "You didn't need Liam's team to keep an eye on Jessup."

Grey suppressed a shiver as she studied Micah. His eyes were colder than normal. Calculating. He didn't need to answer for her to know. Maybe it was a result of spending five years in hiding, of looking for conspiracies and danger in every shadowy corner. "You didn't need your own people to watch Jessup, because you knew every move he was going to make.

"How did he buy you, Micah? What was your price?" There was a gun hidden at the entrance of the safe room. Even if she couldn't get the door closed, and Micah was close enough she didn't think she would, she could grab the gun.

"One of my witnesses used to run with Jessup."

"He saw us together and went to Jessup, who is now blackmailing you."

"I'm sorry, Grey. I don't want to see you get hurt."

"But you care more about yourself."

"Well, yeah. I owe some people money. Jessup's my way out."

"What's he get out of the deal? Other than me on a platter?"

"I know how to make people disappear."

Two steps away and around a corner the gun waited in a hidden push panel of the wall. She figured she'd have about five seconds to get it, flip off the safety and aim. The element of surprise was not working in her favor, so she had to hope his deal with Jessup included her not being dead.

Micah had training on his side, and he knew her skill level since he'd taught her to shoot, but she couldn't *not* try to protect herself.

She reached the corner and lifted a hand as if she was grabbing the wall. Her heart slowed as the final moment of her plan drew closer. Listening became a challenge because the main thing she heard was the thumping of her pulse. "Something tells me he can do that without you."

"I can." Jessup stepped in from the kitchen. Blood dripped from a cut across his cheekbone. Liam wasn't right behind him, which filled her with worry.

Cold gripped Grey's spine. She swallowed as she pressed the panel. It slid inward. She reached in and wrapped her hand around the grip. She was a better shot with her right hand, but they were close enough she could make do with her left.

"In fact—" Jessup turned the gun on Micah, "—I prefer it."

He squeezed the trigger. Blood spattered. Micah's body collapsed into the wall with a thud and then slid down.

Grey's pulse beat so fast it could make an Olympic runner look like the fabled tortoise. She quickly moved the gun out and aimed it at Jessup making sure the safety was off. "I'm not as easy a mark as I used to be."

"Girl, you've been a problem from the beginning."

Weird. He was clearly pissed, but he still sounded like he admired her for being difficult. Moving the gun into her right hand, she asked, "Really? Me?"

"You stole my product, which I let go, until that punched a huge hole in my business. You went into hiding which left me in prison for five years." He waved his gun at Micah who moaned softly from where he sat against the wall. "And do you have any idea what it takes to turn a U.S. Marshal against his own witness?"

"Looks like you did it."

"Yes." He raised his gun a fraction so the barrel was aimed at her head. The man liked his head shots. "But I'm tired of prison, and I'm tired of looking for you."

"I'm tired of being afraid. And I want you out of my house."

The front door slammed open at the same moment a scraping sound came from the kitchen. Liam was moving, but so was someone else.

Jessup's finger twitched. Grey dropped to her knees and pulled the trigger before he could. Blood stained the front of his shirt at his shoulder.

Jessup's gun clattered to the floor. He howled and gripped his wrist. Blood seeped between his fingers as he held his new wound. She'd thought she was aiming for his chest, but he was unarmed now and she'd accept the small victory.

Shaking, Grey didn't lower the gun or sit fully on the floor. She needed to be able to move quickly.

Liam rushed in from her right. The man from the hospital rushed in from the entry foyer. Both men had a gun drawn.

The man from the elevator looked at Grey and shook his head. His eyes were less scary than they'd been in the elevator. His tone, when he spoke, sounded apologetic, and not in an I'm-sorry-I-have-to-kill-you way.

"Things would have been so much easier if you hadn't come back." He looked toward Jessup and frowned. "You should have stayed down."

Liam leveled his weapon on the newcomer. "FBI. Drop it."

Pain lanced Grey's mind. *You should have left it alone.*

Memories snapped free of the barriers holding them back. The scene from five years ago, the part she'd blocked, rushed back.

The storeroom door opened and standing over Jessup's shoulder was a dark, intense man with a hard-set frown. "You should have left it alone, Jessup. This is going to complicate things."

Shaking, Grey rose to her feet, studying the man from a new perspective. "Liam."

"You okay?" Liam moved to her side, never breaking his gaze or aim.

She nodded. "Do you trust me?"

"Of course."

"Then shift your aim to Jessup. He and Micah are the only threats now." Liam did as she requested, but there was no doubt he could re-aim in a flash if it became necessary.

With a slight drop to his chin, the other man bent down and laid his weapon on the floor before him. Keeping his hands up and open, he used a thumb to ease his denim jacket back. Clipped to his belt, a badge identified him as DEA. "I'm Agent Sims. I'm here to help."

Liam watched the man who identified himself as DEA as closely as he watched Jessup. He didn't have the advantage of her memory and the best explanation she could offer was, "He's the reason I'm alive."

Chapter Seventeen

Liam paced the crowded hospital waiting room floor certain he would crash if he stopped moving. He wasn't going to stop moving until Grey was out of surgery and the doctors assured him she would recover. Then, only if he saw her for himself and believed them, would he relax.

Everyone who'd met Grey and Ruby since Grey's return either was in or had been in the waiting room with him. Kami and Lana, Kieralyn and Lori, Ava and Gara, Simon and Breck, Aidan and H. They filled the torture devices called chairs. Tyler and Ian had gone off with DEA Agent Patrick Sims to process the surveillance video from Liam's house.

Jessup could deny his actions all he wanted, but thanks to Madame X Liam had a security system that had recorded everything. With Ian's help, they were processing the audio from outside the house. Nothing escaped Ian's supercharged hearing.

"Grey helped make them." Lana held up a Tupperware container of chocolates when Liam passed. "Want one?"

He shook his head, pivoted on the ball of his foot and continued his path.

"Want me to hug you?" Ava offered with a wink. Her empathic touch wouldn't help. He didn't need to be calmed down. He needed Grey within reach.

He shook his head, pivoted on the ball of his foot and continued his path.

"I could write you a happy ending," Gara, his newly published sister, suggested.

The only happy endings he wanted... Well, his sister didn't have a role. He sure as hell didn't want her orchestrating them.

He shook his head, pivoted on the ball of his foot and continued his path.

"I have an idea," Aidan chimed in.

Liam glared.

"Why don't you pace a hole in the floor," his brother said. "That always helps me."

"You guys are cruel," H said from his chair where he leaned his head against the wall. "Poor guy is distraught and you're poking fun."

"Please," Kieralyn scoffed. "Liam takes great pride in giving us grief. This is just the first time he's been vulnerable."

Liam glanced at their hardest won friend without breaking his pace. "They're right, H. Just be glad they didn't know you well enough to mess with you when you were falling for Ava."

"Falling for and eloping with are two different things," Kami said softly. "We just want to know more about the woman capable of wrapping you so tightly around her finger."

Fortunately, they wouldn't know the worst of her, because her testimony wouldn't be necessary in court. She was no longer the threat keeping Jessup in prison, so she was no longer his target. Agent Sims and Liam were his top contenders, but taking them out still wouldn't cancel out the video.

"Good news," Tyler announced as he and Agent Sims stepped into the waiting room. Ian was right behind them with Bucky Barnes, mostly called Bucky, his new service dog.

"Grey?" Liam asked, dropping into the nearest open chair. His leg immediately began bouncing rapidly.

"Ruby?" Simon asked, sitting up straighter in the chair he'd claimed.

All three men shook their heads. Ian spoke up first. "We have Jessup on tape, outside your house, talking about the hitter's screw up. We now know the shooter to be Thomas Iono."

"From the most-wanted list?"

"Yes."

"Also, Micah activated the voice recorder in his car when he was with Jessup. He got more than enough on tape. Seems he wasn't flipped entirely."

"Bastard shouldn't have turned on Grey at all." The mention of Micah's name was enough to piss Liam off. He gritted his teeth and restrained himself from punching something.

"He might not have if Jessup hadn't found the one chink in his armor," Agent Sims said.

"Why'd he reach out to me?"

Agent Sims spoke up. "He was hoping she'd get scared and decide being here wasn't important enough."

"And when she did, she'd run back to him for protection. Though with her no longer officially in the program he wouldn't be bound by the same restrictions."

Sims confirmed with a nod and waved at everyone in the room. "He didn't plan on all of you closing rank around her."

"We take care of our own," Breck said.

"Even some of us who aren't," Lori added.

"You're Trevor's and that makes you ours," Kami put in.

"That," Sims said with a nod, "is what Micah didn't know how to defeat. So, he played the only card left. He helped Jessup escape."

"What have you been doing for the last five years?" Liam asked Sims.

"I've been taking down one connection after another, weakening Jessup's business. As long as Grey was hidden it was fairly simple."

"Simple?"

"He wasn't on the outside and I was able to limit the information he had access to." Sims shrugged. "There was only one connection I hadn't identified, but with Jessup's escape, he showed himself."

Grey had been raped and nearly killed. She'd been taken from her sister and then had faced a betrayal. Her trust issues were only going to be bigger when she had time to think about it all.

"Mr. Burgess." Nurse Reinhart stepped in and looked around the group.

"How are they?" Liam was on his feet and across the room.

"When can we see them?" Simon was at his side in an instant. The private detective had grown attached to Ruby as quickly as Liam had to Grey.

"Dr. Keiths is with Ruby now. Grey will be in recovery in a few minutes. They're both strong women and things are going smoothly so far."

Liam breathed a sigh of relief that had tears threatening. He was almost too tired to care, but not quite. "When can I see Grey?" Liam asked.

"I can take you to her now, but you have to promise to let her rest."

Liam followed Nurse Reinhart to the recovery room. Energy and nerves rose higher and higher with each step.

And every step closer became heavier and heavier. Grey had wanted an annulment. She'd tried walking enough times and had never said she wanted to stay. She'd been tortured and

189

then she'd had to face her rapist a second time. A gun had evened her odds, but torment was torment.

She hadn't thought herself strong and though he loved her and believed in her, he couldn't block the worry she'd give in to pressure and become addicted again. This time she'd have prescription strength meds to start her off.

No. She had fought her way out from beneath the oblivion of drugs. She'd remember the costs and avoid it again. He would be with her to make sure of it.

Decided, he stepped into the recovery room. His eyes were drawn instantly to the back of the room where she lay in a bed.

His heart pounded harder than it had when he'd seen Iono take aim at her or when he'd been away from her and news was delivered about Jessup's escape.

Her only promise had been that she wouldn't leave until things were cleared up. With the danger eliminated and the surgery done, she only had to recover enough to leave. Other than desire, he had no assurance she would stay.

She turned her head toward him and smiled drunkenly. "Liam," she slurred.

"Grey." He sat on the edge of her bed, careful not to jostle her. "How do you feel?"

"Ready to face a wolf."

"Well, maybe you should wait awhile. At least until you can shoot a man two inches above his heart on purpose." The shot she'd made wouldn't be difficult for someone with real training, but for a woman facing down the man who'd tried to kill her... It had been impressive.

"I wanted to kill him."

"I know the feeling." Liam wanted to go back in time to kill Jessup, Micah and the ass that had outed her to Jessup. "I think we'll have to settle for the way it ended."

"Nope." She rubbed her tongue along her teeth as if she was trying to get something off it, probably that drugged cottonmouth feeling that was so irritating. "It's not ended."

"What's not ended?"

"Liam." Her eyes drifted closed and she slipped back to sleep.

Grey had been pretty amenable given the circumstances they'd been facing the last few days. With drugs coursing through her system, she was incapable of argument. Now would be the time to get her to agree to stay forever, assuming she was awake, but that wouldn't be playing fair. Liam liked watching her fight a fair fight too much to rob her of one.

To make sure he was there when she woke up, he stretched out beside her. He'd thought he would fall asleep the moment he knew she was safe and he stopped moving. He was wrong, because all he could do was watch her.

He watched her eyes move rapidly behind her closed lids. He watched the rise and fall of her chest. He watched her nostrils flare with each breath.

He watched the woman who'd turned his world upside down and formulated his next proposal. It would have to be a damn good one to convince her to give him a chance.

Grey stood on the back porch of Liam's home and shook her head at the transformation Lori and her team from Tulle and Tulips Designer Weddings had engineered.

Tabatha, the one they referred to as the Queen of Venues, had designed a glass type walkway that extended over the zero edge swimming pool. Guests would sit on the lawn, and it would look for all the universe like the bride and groom were standing on water.

It was a fitting visual, because that was how they felt about each other.

Misty, florist extraordinaire, had wrapped the most fragile-looking rosebuds around the strands of twinkle lights that her friend's fiancé, Burton, had strung after building the glass platform.

Lori had designed an amazing gown that had been polished off with the perfect amount of bling, or so stated Darci. Hair and makeup were in the hands of Isabella, a sweet woman who had to buy her clothes from a renaissance festival catalog.

Gisella and Tess were in the kitchen sparring for space while they created masterpieces in the cake and food departments. Kayla wandered around all of them snapping pictures of everything and everyone.

They were noisy and chaotic, raunchy and brazen, and Grey found herself relaxing among them.

"This is going to be a beautiful wedding."

Grey turned to see Liam's mother standing a few feet away. Only a few inches shy of Liam's height, with a slender build and soft curves, Mrs. Burgess had been on hand since Liam had brought Grey and Ruby home from the hospital two weeks earlier. She'd apparently been at the house since the day after the surgery to make sure things were set up for when they were released.

"Only the best, right?"

Mrs. Burgess shrugged. "It was nice of Liam to open the place up for H and Ava."

"Yeah. It was nice, and it was his idea."

Unlike the mothers-in-law horror stories were built on, Mrs. Burgess had stayed in the background, giving Grey space to heal. They'd sat in silence to watch movie after movie. They'd talked amiably while she taught Grey to knit. Grey had walked her through several chocolate dishes. Gorgonzola dolce with dark chocolate, a chocolate soufflé with caramel sauce and lemon drizzles with sunken dark chocolate chunks had been the favorites.

Not once had Mrs. Burgess asked about her past or her future plans. She'd made no mention of grandchildren and though Grey suspected some disappointment that she and Liam hadn't had a traditional wedding, she never said so.

"Do you think a fancy wedding is necessary for a strong marriage?" Grey asked, turning back to look at the view.

"No." Mrs. Burgess moved closer. Her smile was so much like Liam's and her eyes were the same warm brown. "If you ask me, I think too often too much effort is put into the wedding and in the process people lose sight of what's important."

"What's that?"

"That." Mrs. Burgess pointed a little ways away.

Grey followed her gaze and saw Liam crossing the lawn toward them. "I don't understand."

"The way Liam looks at you. The way you look at him. You two can be in a room full of people but when you see each other everyone and everything around you fades away."

"He's pretty great."

"He's said the same thing about you. That is what matters to a marriage. That and honesty."

Mrs. Burgess took Grey's hand in hers and laced their fingers. She didn't hold Grey's hand longer than it took to squeeze once. As smoothly as she'd touched, she released. As Liam grew closer, his mother walked away with a parting, "Tell him what he's doing to you."

It was the first time Mrs. Burgess had offered a touch beyond a handshake at their initial meeting. Its simplicity overtook Grey, because in the simplicity rested something she'd thought impossible.

Tears pooled on Grey's bottom lids and she sniffed. Liam's brow pinched together as he joined her. "You okay? You're not hurting, are you? Mom didn't say anything to upset you?"

Unable to speak, she shook her head. In his silent way, Liam pulled her close and wrapped his arms around her. He'd been careful with her since she'd been released from the hospital.

He held her at night and chased away her nightmares, though they were fading. He kissed her every morning before going to work and every night before going to sleep. He'd run baths for her, cooked for her. He'd even read to her while she'd been in the hospital.

He'd been the definition of sweet. Just like his mother. If their plan was to undermine her willpower and talk her into staying, they were miscalculating. She wasn't a delicate bloom that would wilt or fall off the stem at the slightest breeze. It was important they came to understand that. Especially Liam.

Grey pulled back and looked up at him. "Do you know what today is?"

He dipped his head and whispered seductively along her ear. "It's the day before the wedding that's the day before all these people leave us alone."

"You say that like you might want to be alone with me."

"I always want to be alone with you."

"Yet, it's been three weeks since we've been alone."

"We're alone every night."

"Liam." She shook her head.

"What? If something is bothering you, tell me."

"You want to know? Do you really want to know?" Exhausted with being sheltered and protected, she welcomed the invitation to speak her mind.

"Yes."

"Fine. I went from being guarded by a man who in the end was willing to sell me out for money to being guarded by you. I confronted Jessup and then went into the hospital for surgery. I woke up with you there, and don't get me wrong that was great."

"Doesn't sound like you think so."

"During my hospital stay, my room door opened a minimum of forty-eight times a day. Most days it was closer to seventy-four."

"You counted?"

"There's little else to do in a hospital bed for seven days."

"You said once you liked the idea of close friends."

"I did. And the friends actually didn't annoy me."

He backed up a step and crossed his arms over his chest. His head moved up and down in a slow nod. "I've been annoying you."

"You've been sheltering me like I'm too fragile to do anything for myself." She propped her hands on her hips and glared up at him. She was getting on a roll and wanted to air it all. "Do you know what I wanted to do the day I got out of the hospital?"

"Sleep."

"That's what I came home and did, but it's not what I wanted to do."

"What did you want to do, Grey?"

She waved at the house, frustrated. "I wanted to sit in the kitchen and watch you cook. I wanted to curl up on the couch and watch a movie with you."

"You could have done that."

"No." She shook her head. "I couldn't, because Ruby and Simon and your mother and Gara were here. They, or someone else, has been here every moment of every day since we came home. And then there are the wedding plans."

"They're here to help you while I'm at work. And I'm not going to apologize for letting Ava get married here. This place holds a lot of shitty memories for her. She deserves some happy ones."

"I know, and I appreciate every bit of that. I do. But, Liam, I'm feeling claustrophobic. In your huge house I'm feeling smothered."

"That's crazy."

"Yeah? Even Ruby, who hates to go out, has been out."

"Yeah."

"Look around right this second. How many people do you see?"

He looked around and counted the people in the lawn, setting up for the wedding. "Six."

"You missed your mother watching us from the living room window, which proves my point. I am being constantly monitored. I'm not sure if you think I'm going to keel over and die as a result of the surgery or if you're afraid I'm going to bolt."

"Both," he admitted under his breath.

"Well get over it, damn it."

"You've never said you want to stay." He towered over her, but still he didn't raise his voice or wave his arms in aggravation. "You've never said you want me."

"I asked you one time why you wanted me here."

He nodded.

"You told me if I ever decided I was really ready for the answer you'd tell me."

He nodded.

"Liam, I dare you to send everyone away. Let it be just you and me with no one to watch through windows or listen from the next room. Let it be just you and me so we can talk or yell if we want to. Get rid of your buffers and when you do, if you do, I'll be ready to ask my question again."

Without another word, she turned and walked into the house.

His mother turned from the window and smiled. "That wasn't so hard, was it?"

Grey shook her head with her own smile tugging at her lips. She couldn't have dropped a heavier gauntlet at his feet if she were Thor's sister. The question was whether or not he'd pick it up.

Chapter Eighteen

Every step Grey took away from him was a shaft of agony. She'd just stood before him, taken everything he'd done to help her and thrown it in his face. How she could bitch about his actions in one breath and tell him she appreciated them in the next made no sense. Except she was a woman and that sort of logic was a woman's prerogative.

Watching her through the windows, he watched her smile at his mother. Then he noticed something. His mother was feeling proud, like she always did when she won a match with one of them. And Grey, when she looked at his mom, looked victorious.

"I'll be damned," he muttered to himself.

Grey hadn't been complaining about the help he'd provided. She'd been complaining that he was smothering her, giving her no choices, and she was right. He had taken away every decision she could need to make, because he'd wanted to show her how much he cared.

She'd dared him to send everyone away, which he would do as soon as Ava and H were married and order was restored to his house. No. Their house. She'd called it home in the middle of her rant.

He smiled.

He couldn't take their venue away from them at this point, not that he thought that was what Grey wanted. No, he couldn't give her privacy in the house, but that didn't mean he was out of options.

He met his mother's gaze through the window and sent her one of her own victorious smiles as he pulled his phone from his pocket. She wasn't the only one who could make things happen.

Lori had decided after making chocolates with Grey that she should make confections for weddings. It was a brilliant idea, and one he would use, because there'd been a time when Grey had wanted to be a chef.

After a couple of quick phone calls, he slipped his phone back into his pocket and headed inside.

"Mother." He nodded as he passed his mother.

She nodded in return. "Son."

"You're a troublemaker," he told her as he continued past.

"Only when trouble is what's needed."

He laughed as he ran up the stairs, skipping every other one. He pushed open the door to the room he'd shared with Grey. She looked up, wide-eyed, from the book she was reading. Her whole argument had been about him suffocating her and giving her no choices.

What he was doing was risky, because she could see it as more of the same. It was a gamble he was willing to make.

He stalked across the room, pulled the book from her hand and tossed it on the bed. He swept her into his arms and headed downstairs.

"Hey!"

Yeah. She'd gotten good and fired up. So had he. "You had your turn to speak. I'll have mine."

"This is so not what I did, or had in mind."

"You asked me a question. I'm going to answer it."

"By acting like a caveman?"

He grinned. "You can't dictate how a message will be delivered, Grey."

"You are being ridiculous." She smacked his shoulder. "Put me down."

"No."

His mother opened the door to the garage for him and then pressed the button for the garage door. With a nod toward the convertible, that had its top down though it had been up when he'd gotten home, she chuckled. "Key's in the ignition."

"Mrs. Burgess," Grey pled. "Tell him to put me down."

"He's pretty great, huh?" his mother asked as she closed the door with a wink.

Grey smacked his shoulder again, which only made Liam want to laugh more. At the convertible, he lowered her over the side, not bothering with the door. When she started to scramble out, he dropped a hand on her shoulder. "Stay."

One look in his eyes was enough to quell her fight. At least for the moment. After they were on the road and he didn't have to worry about her bolting, he began to explain. "You wanted me to send everyone away, but I think we both know I can't make that happen until after the wedding."

"I know." She sighed a petulant sigh.

"I can still give you some of what you're asking for."

"This should be good."

The drive was a short one, only ten minutes. It seemed interminable though, because he was getting excited about the idea of being alone with her. Completely alone.

He pulled into the shopping center and parked in front of a vacant storefront. Grey looked from the store to him and frowned. "What are we doing here?"

"I'm explaining." He leaned over, pressed a kiss to the bottom of her jaw and opened her door for her. "If you let me."

"I should give you a time limit," she groused.

He smiled as he joined her by the hood of the car. He took her hand in his and led her to the front door that had been covered with newspapers. It was the only shop in the strip that sat empty.

She stopped, refusing to take another step. "I don't want to be here, Liam."

It was a huge gamble to take her back to the beginning, but he believed she was strong enough to face it, to overcome it. "Give me two minutes inside and if you still feel that way we'll leave."

"Two minutes."

He didn't think it would take that long. He'd gotten to know her pretty well. She froze right inside the door. He stopped with her and kept her hand in his. "The shop's been empty since that night."

She rubbed her chest, but said nothing.

"You've mentioned, more than once, how you'd wanted to be a chef and how you enjoyed working with chocolate." He waved a hand at the displays. "Nasty shit aside, this is where you fell in love for the first time. If you were to want to open a chocolatier shop, it's yours. These cases could be filled with your creations."

"Liam."

"You have an amazing talent, Grey. I haven't signed any papers, so there's no commitment on the line here, but if you want to start over, maybe you'll consider starting over where you began. Where you became the woman you are today. Kind of like Ava and H are by getting married at the house."

She looked up at him with tears glimmering. "I'm not as strong as Ava. I can't allow this place back into my life."

"I disagree with the strength argument." He didn't move toward the backroom. Even he struggled with going into the backroom and seeing where she'd been attacked, so if she couldn't do it he wouldn't force it. "But consider something for me."

"What?"

"When you were last here, you lacked the inner strength to stand against stress. You struggled with drugs and because of that you feel you lost everything."

"Yeah."

"That girl died in this store. A woman walked out, but not just any woman. A one of a kind woman a man considers himself blessed to know."

She shook her head.

"The woman who rose up from the ashes of this place was strong enough to start over in a new city with no friends. Every pressure she failed to overcome when she was here was magnified a hundred times over. She got clean and stayed clean. She stayed away from her sister when she realized what she'd lost, because she knew it was safer that way. Then, she risked everything in a daring move to save that same sister's life."

"This is not what I was asking for."

"Sometimes what we need isn't what we ask for, but if you let me finish maybe you'll get both."

"You're a very pushy man."

He shrugged. "Guess you found a flaw."

She smiled at that. It was the first hint he was winning so he plunged forward. "You were faced with two enemies at one time and were brave enough to pull a gun on them. You didn't freeze. You didn't hide. You didn't run.

"Damn, Grey. I've never been more terrified than I was that night when I came to in the kitchen." It still pissed him off that Jessup had knocked him out, but he refused to dwell on it. "I've never been more fucking proud either."

Her eyes widened. She swallowed.

"You have faced the worst I think life will throw at you, and look at what you've walked away with."

She shook her head.

"You told me you wanted a tight circle of friends rather than a large group of acquaintances. They may be smothering you right now, but you have those friends. You wanted to be a part of something special."

She nodded.

He took her hands in his, facing her. His throat burned with the importance of what he needed to say. "I like to think what you and I have is special. I've never wanted to be with someone more. Even when you're yelling at me or lecturing me. Especially when we're in bed curled close."

Her tears spilled over and slid down her cheeks. He kissed one away, but he didn't release her hands. "You want kids. A family. I can give you that, even if we have to adopt or become foster parents."

"Liam." She sighed jerkily. "Why do you want these things with me? I'm damaged goods."

"I want these things with you, Grey, because you're my wife. More importantly, I want these things with you because I love you. I've loved you from the moment you jumped me in Vegas."

She laughed. "How is that possible?"

"Because in that moment, I saw a woman with an inner strength that meant she'd never be a victim. In that moment, I saw a woman who loved and valued life enough to fight for it." He lifted his hand, keeping hers prisoner, and wiped away a tear. "You jumped me, which jumpstarted my heart, and then you laughed when you realized your mistake. God. Your laugh is magic, Grey.

"You asked why I wanted you to stay. It's because I love you. You were surprised I was willing to go into WitSec with you, even hypothetically. It's because I love you. You're my family and I would do anything to make you happy."

"Anything?"

"Anything." He wiped away more tears from her cheeks. "Even if that's getting you the hell out of here."

Her lips curled into a real smile and she blew out a shaky breath. "Thank you."

She couldn't get outside fast enough, and as soon as they did she drew in a huge swallow of air. When they were back in the car and her breathing had returned to normal, she turned her head on the seat. "Liam."

"Yeah, Grey."

"I'd really like it if you'd make love with me again. It's been too long."

"Name the time and place. If you're up for it, I promise I am."

"Now. Home."

"Everyone's still there."

"We don't have to talk to them, though I'm willing to bet your mom has cleared them out."

He was laughing when he started the car to head back home. He turned around to back out of the spot. She leaned in and kissed him. "I love you the same way. I love being your wife."

Eyes locked with hers, he slipped the car back into Park. His heart stopped beating. The world went silent. His lungs stopped. When life penetrated the haze, it came in a flood that rained from his eyes.

There, in the parking lot of the shop that had set her on the path to him, he pulled her into his lap and kissed her. She'd become his wife two years ago to the day and she'd just given him the most perfect gift.

About the Author

Heart-stopping puppy chases, childhood melodrama and the aborted hangings of innocent toys are all in a day's work for Nikki Duncan. This athletic equestrian turned reluctant homemaker turned daring author is drawn to the siren song of a fresh storyline.

Nikki plots murder and mayhem over breakfast, scandalous exposés at lunch and the sensual turn of phrase after dinner. Nevertheless, it is the pleasurable excitement and anticipation of unraveling her character's motivation that drives her to write long past the witching hour.

The only anxiety and apprehension haunting this author comes from pondering the mysterious outcome of her latest twist.

Nikki loves to hear from her readers. She can be found at all the predictable online places.

Twitter: @NDuncanWriter

Facebook: www.facebook.com/NDuncanWriter

Website: www.nikkiduncan.com

Some couples just click.
Others require a hard hat and a stud finder.

Handcuffed in Housewares
© 2013 Nikki Duncan
Tulle and Tulips, Book 3

Monday mornings have a reputation for sucking, and today is no different for Burton Anderson. One year ago, his "perfect" life full of prestige, money, success and travel crumbled in the glaring light of betrayal.

This morning? *This close* to making his new construction business a success, a date gone awry has left him handcuffed to a toilet in a housewares store. Naked. And the first customer of the day is coming down his aisle.

Planning and shopping for other couples' Big Day is about as wild and crazy as buttoned-up Leigh Schyuler gets. Until she gets an eyeful of Hearth and Home's daily special. He's definitely a "designer" temptation while she's "off the rack".

But there are risks, and then there are *risks*. Burton isn't sure he can once again trust his heart to a woman who holds the power to ruin him. And Leigh discovers too late that indulging in a little no-strings sex is tying her dream of Devoted Love into hopeless knots...

Warning: Contains a hard-hatted, hard-bodied hero who's good with his hands, and a woman who'd like him to build a bridge over her sexual boundaries. Nuts and bolts never had it so good.

Available now in ebook from Samhain Publishing.

SAMHAIN
PUBLISHING

It's all about the story...

Romance

HORROR

www.samhainpublishing.com

CPSIA information can be obtained at www.ICGtesting.com
Printed in the USA
LVOW11s2128130315

430535LV00003B/79/P